Goodreads Reviews for the D…

The Darkening Sky (4.44 Stars)

'Absolutely enjoyed this first novel.'

'I have read many a crime book, but this book was different. I never for one moment guessed how the story would unfold.'

'Loved the way the two main characters (Superintendent Lynch and Dr Power) interacted with one another.'

'Illustrations were brilliantly drawn and brought the characters to life.'

'Thoroughly enjoyed this debut novel from Hugh Greene.'

'Brilliant. Very much enjoyed – a new detective series based in England.'

'This was quite a read. Greene brings a lot to the table in this with great details on psychiatry, forensics, medicine, society, cars, and countless other small details, yet they are delivered with ease and purpose. As for the strengths? For me, the dialogue wins it. It's natural. It has wit without heavy punchlines. Greene handles the reveal superbly and leaves you hanging until the end. Sign me up for more Power and Lynch.'

'It is a good crime and psycholo… reader interested to the end. I l… The Darkening Sky is no excepti… development of characters; I fel… personally. I look forward to fur… entertaining and somewhat edg… to start paying attention to in m… recommended.'

The Fire of Love (4.62 Stars)

'Good plot and enjoyable read – away to locate more books in this series.'

'This is a gripping story, I was hooked from the first page and found it difficult to put down. The description of the house and the man who built it was very true to the time and the author really brings it to life.'

'I love the illustration by Paul Imrie on the cover, it is very striking and beautifully drawn as are the black and white illustrations inside.'

'A well written book with a well-thought out storyline, I enjoyed it very much and definitely want to read the next one.'

'There are lots of twists and turns and complex characters to keep the ending from you and difficult to guess.'

'After the first chapter I could not put it down.'

'The illustrations were brilliant evocations of the Power/Lynch world.'

'I love the little links between the books in the illustrations. Dr Power as drawn is quite dishy. I think I'm falling in love with Dr Power.'

'What I enjoy about Hugh Greene novels are not only the illustrations, but the twists.'

'A good read that I would recommend to anyone who enjoys crime novels and psychological thrillers. The writing is constantly good and interesting.'

The Good Shepherd (4.38 Stars)

'I was attracted by the cover of this book, which I thought very striking and enigmatic.'

'There was drama and suspense and a nice twist at the end. It was quite compulsive, I felt I had to read more to see what happened next.'

'It is a very enjoyable and intriguing read. Well-written, it evokes the spirit of the times, the mid-nineties.'

'I enjoyed this book. The characters were interesting and I felt the book was well researched.'

'The story builds well with excellent attention to detail paid to the places that the main characters visit.'

'The pace of plot was gripping, and makes me want to know what is next. The illustrations were fantastic, and really added to the story.'

'An excellent read, loved it.'

'I was hooked from the first paragraph.'

Also by Hugh Greene

The Darkening Sky
The Fire of Love
The Good Shepherd

Omnibus of Three Novels in a Single Volume
The Dr Power Mysteries

Dr Power's Casebook

Hugh Greene

Illustrated by Paul Imrie

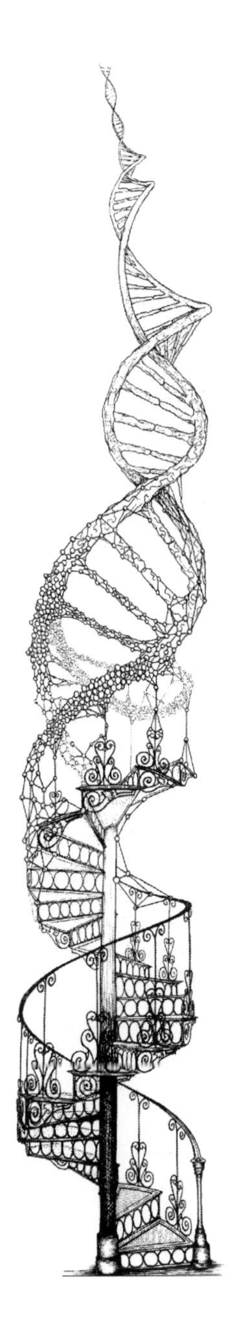

ISBN 10: 1518751601
ISBN 13: 978-1518751608

First Edition Published Worldwide in 2015

A catalogue reference for this book is available from the British Library

Typeset in Cambria
Proofreading and typographic design by Julie Eddles

www.hughgreene.com

twitter: @hughgreenauthor

Contents

Christmas 1993

Snowflakes fell; soft, white, cold and fluffy. The flakes drifted slowly down through the still air to settle on the silent, flat stones of the Edge. The red sandstone escarpment was gradually being carpeted in a white blanket of snow. Under the heavy grey sky whirling flakes swirled round and smothered Thieves Point, Stormy Point and the Wizard's Well.

Castle Rock and Clock House Wood were gradually muffled in a thick, white cloak that stretched far below the high Edge and over the Cheshire plain below. The ancient places of the Edge were silenced.

Dr Power awoke in a tangle of warm and naked legs and arms and luxuriated in the heat of the bed. He pressed Eve's body close to him as she slept by his side. The room was bright and quiet, and he gently eased himself out of the bedclothes and wandered over the carpet to the window and nudged the curtains apart.

Outside, the garden of Alderley House was thick with snow. Virgin, smooth, unmarked in any way, even by the feet of birds. He grinned at the sight, excited, like a boy. Power looked over to Eve. She slept deeply for now, but she had been awake and restless through much of the night. One time he had awoken and from the bed had seen her staring out into the darkness of the night in the chair by the window. Another time he had been awoken by her next to him, crying out in her sleep, arms pushing out at some unseen person or thing from her nightmare. She'd woken then, shuddering, perspiring and panting, and he had asked her about her dream.

"The Barrow," she said simply, in a whisper, and turned away from him.

Now, hours later, on Christmas morning, she had managed to find some rest. And here was Power, agog with his child-like excitement about the snow and Christmas morning. He debated whether to wake her and share his unbridled enthusiasm or whether to let her rest, and decided to defer any decision by making breakfast on a tray. He stole out of the bedroom, along the landing and down the wide flight of stairs to the hall and kitchen.

He switched on the CD player in the kitchen. To the music of Hely-Hutchinson's Carol Symphony, he started assembling dishes of fruit – prunes and apricots – yoghurt and some buttered toast, made with home-baked bread. He loaded the Gaggia coffee machine and brewed coffees and foamed milk to make himself a Latte. Eve liked her coffee dense and black. In a clinical frame of mind Power strayed into a reverie as to whether too much coffee was aggravating her anxiety and her sleep disorder.

Satisfied with the look and contents of the tray, and with Eve's present safely stowed in his dressing gown pocket, Power made his way out of the kitchen. The third movement of the Symphony drifted behind him as he carried the breakfast tray up the thickly carpeted stairs.

Eve was awake. She had showered and sat in a cocoon of snow-white towels. "Had to shower," she said. "Didn't sleep well. Woke up hot and bothered."

"The same dream?"

"Always the same dream."

"I made breakfast. Fruit and yoghurt, toast. Coffee."

"It smells good," she essayed a small smile.

He put the tray on the bed and kissed her, "Happy Christmas."

"Happy Christmas," she said and reached for the syrupy black coffee.

"I bought you this," he said and fumbled in his dressing gown pocket to get a long, slim box in silver wrapping paper and a red bow.

"Oh," she sounded surprised, but in a good way. "Aren't we opening presents by the tree?"

"This one's special and portable," said Power.

It was a heavy silver bracelet, sparkling with some diamonds. It took her breath away. The thought that she loved Power very much crossed her mind, but she felt removed from that world, detached. She had been for months. Eve looked up at Power and signalled her pleasure with a smile. She had felt so far apart from everyone for months. Now, at this movement, the thought of making love appeared and disappeared. She wondered at how understanding Power could be. Did his profession lend him extra patience? She didn't want to feel like a charity case or one of his patients.

"It's lovely," she said. "I'll wear it after lunch. Speaking of which, we'd better get started on that."

"We can relax," said Power. "We've only just had breakfast."

"Oh, we can't break the traditions of Christmas Day," she tutted. "What would happen?" And she dressed quickly and fled downstairs, Power following in her wake.

In the kitchen, Power trawled through the fridge for the turkey crown for two, bacon, potatoes, carrots, sprouts, chestnuts and assembled all the festive paraphernalia of Christmas lunch. Eve busied herself helping him. Normally Power liked cooking himself. This year she wanted to keep busy and listened to Power's music as she peeled green leaves of sprouts and cut their bases with a cross. The ritual was comforting. She asked Power, "Don't you ever go to church at Christmas?"

"I leave church to those like Andrew Lynch," said Power looking at the Christmas card on the windowsill from his friend, Superintendent Lynch and his wife.

“When I was a child we always went to Midnight Mass, and Church on Christmas morning. We’d take our toys and sit there. Then lunch. And then the aunts would descend like fat doves from a tree and settle down for tea.”

And then the carrots were chopped, the sprouts and chestnuts peeled, and sitting in pans ready to boil. The turkey and roast potatoes were in the oven. The air was full of the scent of spice; cloves in the bread sauce, cinnamon in apple sauce. Power poured them two large glasses of Fino sherry. “Presents? From under the tree?” he suggested.

“Presents for you, maybe,” she said. “I’m not sure I deserve any more.”

In the living room, Power set a match to the log fire, which soon crackled into bright flames. He knelt by the Christmas tree. Some fallen needles prickled his knees. The scent of the pine sap was strong. A small cache of presents had been placed under the tree. He reached for one and handed it to Eve. “No, she said. “It’s your turn to open one.”

He opened one of her presents to him – some long-sleeved shirts.

And so they went back and forth for some minutes; opening books, CDs, chocolates, bottles of wine. At last one present remained.

“Your main present, Carl,” she said.

He could smell the oil paint and varnish before he opened it. It was a painting she had done. A landscape; snow stretching into the distance, purplish ice depicted under a red sky. Two lonely fir trees poked through the ice and snow, seemingly hundreds of yards apart.

"Just right for today," said Power nodding through the window at the garden festooned in white. “How did you know it was going to be a white Christmas?”

She laughed softly, “Do you like it?”

Power nodded and gave her a kiss.

The phone rang, and Eve went to put the vegetables on to boil.

It was Power's father. "Are you awake? I didn't wake you?"

"No, Dad. We've been up for ages."

"Eve's there?"

"Yes."

"I just wanted to ring and say Happy Christmas to you, Carl. All the best. I love you, you know?"

"I know Dad," said Power. "I'm sorry we couldn't be with you."

"Never mind, maybe next year?"

After the phone call, there was lunch. This was a protracted affair and there was much good food to warm and cheer Power's heart. There was laughter. There were crackers and party hats. There were party poppers that fired paper streamers in the air, to fall and congeal in the gravy or drape languidly over the turkey. There was a plum pudding with purple flames of fiery brandy. But Power drank only one glass of wine. "I think I'm on call," he confessed to Eve.

She raised her eyebrows. "Oh Carl! You didn't say. Why do they always put you on-call at Christmas?"

"For my sins," said Power. "Which must be many." Seeking for a distraction, he looked outside at the snow. "Shall we go and make a snowman?"

Eve was frowning. "We're not children, Carl."

"We could have children though," said Power. And on the fulcrum point of that sentence the whole tone of the day revolved and shifted, changing irrevocably. The day spun away from him, out of his control.

"You know I don't want to," said Eve. "You know that." She stood up; brittle faced, holding something in, forcing herself to smile. "You go and play in the snow, Carl. It's all right. I'll put the coffee on."

Feeling somewhat foolish now, a small knot of anxiety gnawing away deep inside. Power put on his coat and hat, and feeling diminished to the point of boyhood, slipped outside into the garden and went through the motions of building a snowman. He rolled the snow into three balls – large, medium and small – and stacked them up. Branches for arms and stones for eyes, the snowman stared at the kitchen window. But neither Power nor the snowman caught a glimpse of Eve.

Snowman complete, Power followed his tracks in the snow, back into Alderley House. He stomped his feet, and the snow fell from his shoes. He changed into slippers left by the rear porch and went to find Eve. She was watching the Queen's Christmas Broadcast and nursing a mug of black coffee. She nodded silently to the tray where his mug stood alone.

"Thank you," said Power.

Silence.

"Carl?" Eve summoned his attention. "I've been thinking, for a while now. About how you want children, and I don't. Not now. Probably not ever."

"It's to do with what happened," said Power. "It'll pass. It will heal."

"And one day, when it's too late, and you realise finally that I've stopped you having children. What then? What then for us, for me and you? Isn't it better to realise it now and go our . . ."

"Don't do this now," said Power. "Not now, not today. I didn't mean anything when I said . . ."

"I'm not sure that there is a 'right' time for these things," said Eve. "Maybe I won't always feel this way. Maybe things can be different some day for us. But we all have our journeys to make. And maybe our journeys are . . . you know, different ones."

Power felt his eyes prickle and grow moist. He felt his stomach suddenly reel and fall like it had become a lead weight in his belly. For a moment his vision seemed to close about him, and he felt remote and somehow stretched thin and then he heard the phone ringing.

Eve touched his arm, "It's the phone Carl. You're on call."

Power stumbled into the hall and found he was answering in an automatic way. "Dr Power, can I help you?"

"Dr Power?" A young female voice echoed out of a hospital room somewhere. "It's Dr Snowden. I'm an SHO calling from Withington Hospital. We can't get in touch with our consultant today, and you are the only consultant we can reach in the North West. We're desperate for an urgent opinion on a patient in casualty here. Do you want me to tell you about her?"

"I'm on my way," said Power. "I'll be about 45 minutes."

He put the receiver down and smiled wanly at Eve, who stood by the living room door. She helped him on with his coat. "Are you all right to drive, Carl?"

He nodded and fumbled in his coat for his car keys. He wondered if the car would start in the cold. He checked he had his bleep with him and picked up his on-call bag with his pens and papers inside.

"I'll be a couple of hours at Withington," he said. "Will you be here when I get back?"

She interrupted before he could say anything else. Her voice was firmer than his, "I'll phone you, Carl. In the next few days."

He nodded. He felt cold even though he was still in the warmth of the house. He couldn't look her in the eye as he made his way outside. She watched him clearing snow from the car. Uncharacteristically, the engine started first time. She watched him edge out of the drive and down the road on the snowy hill beyond.

The village lay covered in white below the Edge. Power motored cautiously along the high street. Under a tree stood a lone piper playing a tune called Solstice Bells. He stopped for a moment when he saw Power's battered car and waved to Power as he passed. Power nodded, wondering to himself whether the piper had a warm place to stay.

Up the hill at Alderley House, Eve finished the washing up. She checked that the oven and hob were safely out. She switched off the living room lights but left the Christmas tree lights on. Eve decided to leave the hall lamp on, in case it was dark when Power returned.

All this done; Eve locked the front door. She wondered whether to push the copy of the house keys Power had given her through the letterbox. She decided not to. There was time yet.

She looked up at the house she thought that she was leaving for the last time, trying to fix it in her memory.

"We all have our own journeys to make," she whispered to herself. Her voice sounded strangely muffled because of the snow.

The night was drawing near.

The clouds in the leaden dusk sky began to disgorge fresh flakes of snow that fluttered and dwindled down to earth.

Delirium

13th March 1994

Dr Power felt himself being carried along by the noisy crowd as it bustled and flowed like a stream of red soldier ants through the streets of Anfield. The flow moved inexorably towards the stadium. Power looked out of place in a corduroy jacket and tie and so he bought a red scarf from a roadside stall, just so he could try and blend in. The afternoon air was filled with the sound of shouted anthems and buzzing with enthusiasm. Power held onto the ticket in his pocket and tried to see his way towards the turnstiles for the Kop. He was finding it difficult to think clearly and his early excitement about going to the game was now tinged with the anxiety generated by being a fish out of water.

Power had supported Liverpool in a tentative fashion since childhood. His grandfather, a staunch supporter since his own boyhood, had been mortified by Power's lukewarm enthusiasm for the game. His grandfather had stood on the Kop as a supporter week in and week out for decades. This was Dr Power's first visit to see the match in person. He was hurried through the gates by the crowd and up onto the Kop itself, and the Stadium view opening below him was suddenly a vast and awe inspiring spectacle. He gasped at the vastness of the stands, the green spread of the pitch and the red and blue patchwork of the fans. There was a mixed smell of beer, hot pies and disinfectant. And the noise of the crowd; shouting and singing.

Power had once worked at the Royal Liverpool Hospital as a trainee, and now with a free weekend had decided to return to work there as an on-call locum consultant. The agency had told him it was not a busy job and that he might only be called 'once or twice' during his sixty-four hours on duty over the weekend. He had been given a small flat in the hospital to sleep in. True enough, to the agency's promise Power had been called only once or twice and it was now Sunday. The ticket for the match had come to him from Roly, the hospital porter, who could always be relied on to source such things.

It was Derby day; when the city's two football teams squared up to each other and played with pride and hoped for ascendancy over their rival. Power watched the blue and red players emerge onto the pitch and almost felt caught up in the emotion of the crowd as they roared and competed in song. Power mumbled and stumbled his way through the words to 'You'll Never Walk Alone' and even waved his scarf aloft along with those around him. When the singing was done and the scarves and banners were temporarily lowered, Power saw that the match had already begun and the crowd's attention was focused on the ball as it flicked around the pitch. Everton scored early and Power felt the corporate groan of the Kop viscerally. As the ball rocketed back and forth Power was conscious of the crowd swaying to gain better sight and he was carried from side to side, to and fro. Seconds later Rush scored, levelling the score. The open-mouthed Everton supporters were stunned into silence and the Kop erupted into joyous song. Power thought of his grandfather caught up in this crowd and wondered how he had never joined in with the old man's passion. Power watched as eighteen-year-old Robbie Fowler scored a second goal and the first half came to a close. He became aware of a sudden vibration in his pocket and swore. The bleep was going off. With the press of the crowd he struggled to extract the bleep. The small grey screen showed the number he was to call: 0151 706 2000 – the Royal.

Dr Power, with many mumblings of 'excuse me, excuse me', negotiated his difficult way through the banners, scarves, arms, and bodies that were obstacles to his progress. Cursing, he tried to find a payphone in the concrete bunkers and corridors behind the stands so that he could phone the hospital switchboard. Above him the game continued and he could still hear the distant clamour of the supporters.

Power pushed 10 pences into the belly of the only payphone he could find and dialled the Royal: 706 2000. A lady on switchboard answered, "Royal Liverpool."

"It's Dr Power, Locum Consultant Psychiatrist, you bleeped me?" Somewhere above, there was a roar from the crowd about a missed goal.

"It's Stephanie on Switchboard, Dr Power. You're back with us then?"

"Just for the weekend."

"I remember when you were a Senior House Officer here. Do you remember when I phoned you about my father?"

"Yes, yes, I do." He remembered that she had phoned him a few years ago in the middle of the night when he was sleeping. He remembered that he had had to try and control his annoyance, but something had made him answer her questions.

"We took your advice. And he's a lot better now. So thank you, Dr Power. I'll put you through now. Your senior house officer on call wanted you. Nice to hear your voice again."

Power waited till another voice came on the line, young and female. "Hello, Dr Power. This is Dr Ambrose. Please can you help with some advice? I was asked to see a lady on the medical ward this morning and I gave some advice, but they aren't happy with that and they want a senior opinion."

"Tell me about the case."

"It's a seventy-five year old lady on ward 6X who they referred as a 'sudden case of schizophrenia'. She was hallucinating and accusing the nurses of the night shift of holding a black mass. When I saw her she was disorientated and delirious. I advised them to find the medical cause."

"That sounds fair enough," said Power. "She's the wrong age for developing schizophrenia and really an acute brain syndrome is most likely. What's the problem?"

"She barricaded herself in the bathroom at lunchtime and when the nurses forced their way in she threw things at the nurses, now they want her off the ward."

"But that could be a death sentence if she's transferred to a psychiatric ward without anyone treating the underlying problem. Have they excluded a chest infection or a urinary tract infection?"

"No, they . . ."

The payphone started beeping. It wanted more of Power's change. But there was none in his pocket. An automatic voice advised him he had only thirty seconds left. Too little time for him to sort the complex problem over the phone.

"I'm coming in," he said. "Don't do anything until I'm there." He put the receiver down and cursed softly. He began his descent down the stadium stairs to the turnstiles. The streets around the stadium were quiet and in contrast to how they had been before the match. Everyone was inside Anfield and focused on the match. Power hailed a taxi to the Royal. He had to leave the match halfway through. He felt somewhat bereft and thought of his grandfather.

"Leaving at half-time are you?" observed the taxi driver. "Everton supporter leaving in disgust?"

Power tried to show the red scarf he was wearing, but the taxi driver was too focused on the road to see. "I'm on call," he said. "I've had to go in. First match I've ever been to."

"Go away, boss. First match?"

"Standing in the Kop, like my Grandad did."

"They'll be putting seats in there later this year. No-one standing there any more. All that history gone. After Hillsborough. You know?"

Power thought back. He'd been on-call then too. Remembered the survivors coming back from Sheffield. He'd seen patients at the Broadgreen Hospital casualty. The first hospital at the end of the M62 and the surviving supporters' first port of call on their return to their hometown. "Aye," he said. "Safer, I suppose." Power's eyes prickled with tears and he was surprised by his unexpected emotion.

Power looked up and caught the cabby's eyes looking at him in the mirror. The driver had noticed Power's eyes welling up with tears. "Don't worry. You're not alone."

The taxi drew up at the entrance to the Stalinesque concrete building, which was the current incarnation of the Royal Liverpool Hospital. It had replaced the elegant brick-built edifice designed by Waterhouse, which had somehow escaped demolition and mouldered a few hundred yards away, unused since the seventies. Power was familiar only with the new Royal, having trained as a junior doctor in the concrete cavern of a building.

He paid the driver and ran into the entrance hall passing Roly the porter who was taking someone in a wheelchair to X-ray from Accident and Emergency. "Shouldn't you be at the match, Doc?"

"Called in," Power shouted back.

"What timing, eh?" said Roly, shaking his head.

Power turned left out of the hangar-like entrance hall and hammered the call button at the lift shaft.

Dr Ambrose was standing outside ward 6X. She was tall with long blonde hair and her turquoise-blue eyes were chock full of worry. In her left hand she had a notebook and pen; she held out her other hand as he approached. "Dr Power?" He nodded. "Oh, thank goodness. I'm Anne. We spoke on the phone."

"I thought I'd better come in. I ran out of money for the pay phone."

"I'm so sorry, Dr Power, but you may have had a wasted journey."

"Why? Surely the patient is still alive?" He had seen similar confused patients on medical wards simply arrest.

"I hope so," said Dr Ambrose. "But she's not on the ward for you to review any more." She saw Power frowning and hurried to make things clearer. "She's left. Absconded. And I wrote it in the notes, as clear as day. That she was to be observed at all times. But she's just been allowed to wander off." It was not unheard of, why would a confused person that didn't know why they were in hospital, or indeed know that they were in a hospital, stay there?

"When was this?"

"I don't know. The nurses don't seem very clear so they can't have been observing her properly. I only saw Mrs Carey this morning round 11 o'clock. They phoned me again to see her about half an hour ago. Then I phoned you straight away. And I came over here from the accommodation and when I got here she'd gone."

"What did you talk about with her? Were there any particular themes?"

"She wasn't happy. She was convinced the nurses were witches. She'd seen them clustered round the bed of another patient at night and misinterpreted it as some kind of Satanic sacrifice. She said she'd seen little devils dancing round them. She wanted to complain. She said she'd take it to the top."

Power frowned. "To the top?" His eyes flicked over to the lifts, which were near the ward doors. "And she was seeing little things . . . devils?" Dr Ambrose nodded. "Did she see any while you were there?"

"She kept looking over at the corner of the room, near another patient's locker. And smiling at someone or something."

"What was she in hospital for? And how long has she been in?"

asked Power.

"She came in a three days ago. For a lung biopsy."

"And how much was she drinking before she came in?"

"I didn't ask," said Dr Ambrose.

"Did anyone ask Mrs Carey? When she was first clerked in?"

"I can go and ask the nurses and look in the notes," Dr Ambrose offered this to propitiate Power. She sensed he was annoyed. On reflection it was such a basic thing, to take an alcohol history in a case of confusion. She felt ashamed.

"In a minute," said Power. "Tell me, what does she look like?"

"Small. Thin. Looks older than her years. White hair. White nightie."

"Okay," said Power. "You go and check out the notes about the alcohol history. I guess they will have neglected to take a proper history too." He looked directly at her eyes and into her soul. "You won't make that mistake again, will you?" She shook her head. "Tell them to alert the porters to search every floor of the hospital. And alert the police in case she tries to walk home in her nightie. It has been known. Now, can I just check – Mrs Carey said she was going to go to the top about the nurses and their black mass?"

Dr Ambrose nodded.

"Okay," said Power. "Go. I'll call you later."

Power summoned the lift and was grateful when it arrived, empty. He held the door open while he studied the list of wards and floors. The various wards and departments were all listed for floors one to nine. There was nothing beyond the ninth floor. And yet there were clearly ten buttons, a vertical row of ten black and white buttons set into the silver steel of the left wall, one for each of floors one to ten.

Power pressed the button for the tenth floor. The lift's doors swished to, enclosing Power in the lift's metal cell. The lift began to ascend.

The doors opened onto a standard hallway, but there were no signs to guide the visitor to any wards. A single red and white sign stood on a small easel and said 'Floor not in General Use'. Power had never been here before. He felt somewhat disorientated himself. The deserted floor's silence was almost complete.

The lino floor outside the lift was covered in fine dust. Power felt a surge of hope when he saw the dust had been disturbed. If he looked closely he could see small footprints made by a bare human foot.

He thought it would now be easy to follow the trail and find Mrs Carey and return her to the ward. However, when he pushed through the swing doors out of the lift area, where the concrete floors of the corridors had barely been touched since the building was built twenty years before, the footsteps were no longer visible.

The tenth floor had been left largely unfinished. A vast expanse of bare and empty, flat grey concrete, stretched from the windows at the front of the building to the windows at the rear.

On one wall someone had built some boxes that were meant to function as offices. These were locked and labelled 'Liaison'. He felt sorry for whoever they had intended to work up here in this lonely eyrie on this abandoned floor. The view from the windows ran far over the city. He could see the towering bulk of both Cathedrals, the light twinkling on the Mersey and the ferries plying back and forth. Power wished he had binoculars with him.

There was a partition of chipboard sealed with gaffer tape stretching across where he knew the link section to be. The Royal was arranged in a grim quadrangular way about a dark and depressing central atrium. He could see the Medical School building across the way, and the link building between the wards and the academic centre was the one that was screened off.

Power glanced around the empty floor. Mrs Carey couldn't be hiding here. There was nowhere to hide. And if the footsteps were hers then they represented only a single journey forwards. There was no return journey documented in the dust. Logically Mrs Carey had left the empty floor. Power could only look for her exit and the only candidate for such an exit was a door in the chipboard partition.

The door was marked 'No Entry!' Power tried the handle. The door was unlocked, but there was considerable pressure to his advance. He had to really push to open the door. He half-wondered whether Mrs Carey's unconscious body lay immediately behind the door, but it was merely the pressure of air. He felt a strong and constant rush of cold air through the gap. Power forced his way through and began to doubt that Mrs Carey, described as she had been as a small and frail old lady, could have summoned the strength to get through this portal.

Power heaved against the door, squeezed through the gap and the door slammed to behind him.

The space beyond the partition was, if anything, even more unfinished than the space Power had left behind. Piles of unused building materials; wood, bags of cement, and panes of glass on pallets lay scattered about. There was probably plenty for Mrs Carey to complain about on her quest to take things 'to the top'. There were numerous heavy and filmy sheets of plastic hung from the roof space, presumably to dampen the whirling wind. Over on the right hand side of the space the cause for the excessively turbulent air became clear. There were at least three large window bays that were gapingly devoid of glass. Through these, the whirling Atlantic wind whistled its way in to the building's void. Beyond the empty window bays there was sturdy scaffolding, a perilous ten floors above the ground.

There, on the edge of nowhere, stood a woman in a thin, white cotton nightdress, which the wind had plastered, tautly to her tiny form. She was looking out over the city, her hair streaming behind her.

Power hated heights.

He approached her gradually, partly not to frighten her, but also to try and acclimatize himself to his fear. He called out rather tentatively, "Mrs Carey?"

She turned slowly. Power could see that she was holding onto the single railing that stood between her and a fall to the ground ten stories below the planking on which she stood. Power noted, with a lump in his throat that there were thin gaps between the planks. As he approached the window space he could see straight through the gaps.

"I've been waiting for you; quite frankly this place is a mess."

"My name is Dr Power. I'm a doctor."

"Well, what do I need one of those for? I'm fine." She paused. "And your friend says so too."

"My friend?"

"There," she pointed to a space somewhere beside Power's left hip.

"What does he look like?" asked Power, moving gingerly onto the planking, testing it first with his foot before he placed any weight on it.

"Well, I don't like to say in front of him, but I'm sure he knows he's a dwarf. In a white coat."

"Ah," said Power, wondering whether he was in any position to start challenging Mrs Carey about the nature of the hallucination she was having. The academic portion of his mind was classifying her hallucination as Lilliputian. "What does he say?"

"Can't you hear him? Or ask him yourself?"

"If you can help me understand, please? What does he say?"

"He says I can trust you."

Power felt a degree of relief. "Shall we go inside to talk? It's a bit windy here."

"No, I like it here. It's too stuffy in that place. They've got the heating far too high for a fashion shop. No-one will buy any clothes if they feel warm. I like it here on deck."

"Do you think we are on a cruise or something?"

"Just about to set sail for the Med." Suddenly she sat down and dangled her legs over the edge of the planking. "Come and join me, I'm sure the Captain won't mind. And maybe, if we're lucky, the Steward will bring us some drinks."

Very carefully indeed, Power inched over the wooden boards and sank down onto his knees. He felt a little better closer to the planking. He sat back from the edge though, with his back to a concrete pillar between the window bays. She frowned at him. "Come here and dangle your legs in the sea breeze, it's so delicious on your toes."

"I feel safer here," said Power.

"Oh, you're no fun," she said. "You'll never grow old, Doctor, because you're not even alive. Although," she winked at him. "As the ship's doctor I suspect that you have your share of the ladies." She nodded at Power's imaginary dwarfish colleague. "He says you do, too." She laughed a high bell-like laugh.

"Do you like a drink?"

"Oh thank you, I'll have a brandy and soda, please."

"No, I meant how much do you drink?"

"I haven't had anything in this place. The worst cruise ever. If I see the Captain I have many things to say about his ship. Orgies and black masses on the lower decks, and up here as dry as a Welsh Sunday."

Power tried again, "I'm wondering if that's the problem. That

ROYAL

you stopped drinking when you came here. Do you drink every day at home? How much?"

She viewed him suspiciously and pursed her lips defiantly. "No more than a bottle a day. It's medicinal, you know."

"Of brandy?" She nodded. "Can you recall how you got up here?" He was testing to see if she could remember. His eyes were taking in other signs. There was a tremor of her hands when she touched her face. She had slightly dilated pupils. The old lady had delirium tremens.

"I climbed the gangplank, with your dwarf friend dancing a jig."

"And what did you do this morning?"

"Deck quoits. I won a prize," she said somewhat smugly.

Power deduced she was confabulating. Mrs Carey's morning had been spent on the respiratory ward talking to Dr Ambrose, and not on some illusory cruise ship. "Shall we go in now?" he asked. "It's a bit cold out here isn't it?"

"Your friend says there will be dancing. I can hear the band starting up." Although there was just the afternoon sound of the city, Mrs Carey thought she heard a swing band. She moved to stand up, grew unsteady and wavered close to the edge. Power gasped. Mrs Carey giggled. "Oops, tiddly again. Nearly went overboard."

Power decided to lie shamefacedly. "Let's go inside," he said. "We can have a drink at the bar and then dine at the Captain's table. Come on, take my arm."

"Ooh yes, thank you, your manners are as handsome as your face . . . I'm afraid I've forgotten your name."

"Dr Power," he said.

"The ship's doctor," she murmured as they passed from the scaffolding into the building. Here, her legs crumpled suddenly from under her, but there was a second set of arms to join Power in assisting her. Not a hallucinated pair of hands either, but the capable hands of Roly the Porter.

“Is this where you take all your lady friends, Dr Power?” Roly asked, smiling. “Come on, let’s get you back Mrs Carey.”

The light was fading now, and the air on the tenth floor was chill, and the wind was becoming keener. Together, Dr Power and Roly half carried, half escorted Mrs Carey from the deserted tenth floor into the light and warmth of the hospital.

“How did you know where I was?” asked Power.

“A little bird told me. Dr Ambrose thought you headed this way.”

“It’s been quite a day,” said Power. “I thought I might lose her over the edge.”

“Never mind,” said Roly. “All’s well that ends well, don’t they say? And you saw the best of the match. The final score was 2-1.”

The Dark
June 1994

Power had been in the garden of Alderley House all day. He had rested under the trees in the Saturday sun; head occasionally nodding and consciousness drifting like a raft in the Southern Seas. The air was clear. There was the sound of bees humming in the flowers nearby and birdsong. In the far distance, he could hear the music from the Traveller camp. They played 'Asylum' and 'Passing of Time' by The Orb, and 'Setting Sun' by The Chemical Brothers, in a loop. The Travellers had been gathering over the last few days and were now waiting on the Edge, as they did every year now, for the Solstice which was next week. Mostly, they had been respectful. Only a few had traipsed over his land. Once or twice Power thought he had glimpsed the figure of the Piper through the trunks of oak and Scots pine. Dr Power mused on a book of poetry from his library; reading and re-reading one line in particular that he liked – 'For the sun has stippled the pear and polished the apple'. Occasionally through the afternoon Power hummed to himself rather like a bee.

Now it was late, the Traveller camp was winding down for the night and Power, soothed by the heat and dreamy with the scent of Summer, had retired to bed upstairs. He had the windows and curtains wide open and from his bed could see the stars slowly whirling in the night sky.

Power slipped slowly and imperceptibly into sleep, but woke suddenly. Moonlight streamed into his room, and he felt suddenly afraid. There was the sound of laughter nearby. Two voices. One voice was tinkling and light, the other voice heavy and seemingly jeering. They seemed so very close. Power felt the hairs on his neck prickling. He pushed the duvet aside and gently padded over to the window and looked outside into the garden. He couldn't see anyone there. He did, however, see the flash of white from a badger's coat as it moved stolidly through the undergrowth, foraging.

There was a burst of further laughter, and from where he was next to the window he could now isolate the noise and know it wasn't from the garden in front of him. Perhaps he should try a window on the other side of the house. Power left his bedroom and walked along the landing, his toes felt the soft thickness of the carpet, but he took no comfort alongside his anxiety. The windows on the other side of the house yielded no glimpse of any trespasser. His garden was empty, and the laughter seemed as if it came from within the house.

Power thought of shouting out or of making some noise to frighten any intruders away, but he thought better of it, and wrapped in a blue dressing gown and carrying a cricket bat, he descended the Victorian stairs as silently as he could, given their propensity for creaking.

But by now the laughter had stopped, and the rooms downstairs were empty and still. He moved from room to room, checking each in turn to reassure himself. He checked that doors and windows were locked. All was as he had left it. There was no one in the house except him.

In the morning, Power was glad to leave the house to join a friend's family in Mobberley for Sunday lunch. On his return that evening he searched the garden to the sounds from the nearby Hippy camp. There was no sign of anything unusual.

That night, however, he woke to hear the same sounds, seemingly within his house, excited laughing. There was the sound of someone running past. Power undertook the same fruitless inspection of the garden from the first floor windows and the same fruitless tour of the downstairs rooms. A puzzled Dr Power wondered if he had become ill and was hallucinating, but he comforted himself with the thought that the experiences had been fleeting and isolated, unlike the persistent torment of true hallucinations endured by his patients.

After a sleepless two nights, Power was tired at work on Monday and worked on autopilot through a ward round and a clinic. In the late afternoon he stopped in Wilmslow on his journey home to Alderley village and parked outside Jones' shop to pick up the Farrow and Ball paint and wallpaper he had ordered.

He had been planning to start work himself on refreshing the walls in the kitchen, but after unloading the Saab and piling the supplies on the Ruabon kitchen floor tiles, he realised he was too tired from lack of sleep and slumped at the kitchen table with a pot of Darjeeling tea, and a generous slice of plum cake.

After twenty minutes, he had completed the crossword from that morning's *Guardian* newspaper. The cake was finished. The almost empty teapot stood on the oak kitchen table in front of him with a thin layer of congealing Darjeeling inside its belly.

Refreshed, he thought he would make a start on his project by clearing any furniture away from the walls and into the centre of the kitchen. Opposite him was the largest and heaviest object, a huge pine dresser, almost black with age. The dresser had come with the house, it was three large drawers wide, with a vast rack for plates above, and standing some eight-foot tall. Power began by emptying the drawers of cutlery and the plate rack of crockery. He piled things up on the kitchen table. In one drawer, he came across a small box with an oxidised silver oval in it on a chain. It had once been a 'season ticket' for the trains at the railway station when it had first been built. One had been given free to the first owner of Alderley House to celebrate the development of the village. Power put it with the other debris on the kitchen table. In another drawer he came across a cluster of two rusted keys that seemed unfamiliar. None looked like the keys he used everyday at Alderley House.

He looked at the empty dresser and wondered whether he could move it on his own. It was vast and took up the whole central part of that wall. He took hold of one end of the dresser, braced himself and strained with all his might. The dresser moved barely an inch. Probably the dresser had not been moved in decades. He decided he'd better try something else or ruin his back. He set up a lever and fulcrum under one end of the dresser and very gently raised it a few inches while at the same time sliding a heavy-duty rug under both feet. He repeated the technique at the opposite end of the dresser until the feet at each end were on top of one of the two rugs. Then he was able to slide (still with appreciable effort) the great dresser inch by inch into the centre of the kitchen, away from the wall he wanted to paint.

It was nearly 9 o'clock. Panting away, and determined to do no more work that night, Power poured himself a Pilsner beer and fried himself some Simpson's sausages and placed them into a sausage sandwich with some home-made green chutney. He munched this thoughtfully and inspected the wall. It would need much cleaning as it was covered in the waxy grime of a kitchen wall that hadn't been re-decorated in decades. Then Power noticed something unexpected.

In the middle of the space on the wall where the dresser had stood was the traced outline of a six-foot high rectangle.

Power noted that the edge of the rectangle had been thickly papered over and painted with lime whitewash. He knocked the wall around the rectangle – solid brick and plaster. And in the middle of the rectangle a heavy wooden sound, hollow like an echoing drum. Power started picking at the thick edge of wallpaper that ran down the centre of the rectangle. It resisted his prying fingernails, and

Power went to get the wallpaper steamer, all thoughts of rest dispelled by curiosity.

Half an hour later the kitchen walls and windows were running with rivulets of condensed steam. The kitchen floor was covered with long, thick, soggy and slimy ribbons of paper. The rectangle now facing Power was a made of a serried row of pinewood planks. Someone many years ago had deliberately covered up a doorway.

Power felt stupid. How long had he been living in the house? He walked out of the kitchen into the hall and looked at the wall that led down to the dining room. He paced out the length of the dining room and looked at the space he had left over. There was an unaccounted space between the dining room and the kitchen. The boarded-up opening could lead to a room-sized space. A missing room, here, in his house.

Power returned to the kitchen and stared at the planks for a full five minutes, trying to decide what to do next. The room beyond had probably been blocked up for decades. What for? What lay on the other side of the boards? He thought through all the things that could be in there.

He disappeared off into the garage again and retrieved a heavy crowbar.

Now armed with the crowbar, he stood again in front of the boards and wondered what to do. He could, for instance, just paper over the boards again, paint everything over and forget that which had been hidden.

But now that Power knew, could he ever forget?

It was now 10 o'clock and Power decided that he could not begin to sleep without pressing ahead. He inserted the edge of the crowbar into a gap between two of the planks and wrenched sideways with all his might. The old wood splintered and snapped outwards, one pointed shard hovering close to Power's chest. He put the crowbar in a second time and two planks fell outwards. One by one the planks fell outward and he stacked them up in a corner of the kitchen. Under the planks was a doorway. A white oaken door had stood stoutly behind the planks; unopened by anyone for many years.

Power dropped the crowbar with a clatter.

Guessing that whatever space beyond would be unlit he rummaged in the cupboards for a storm lamp. He found a box of matches on the kitchen table. He struck a match and lit the lamp before restoring the glass cover. He put the matchbox down again. Growing cold after the heated exertion of the evening was over, Power put his jacket back on, gathered up the lamp and returned to the door.

The handle to the door turned easily enough and opened inwards. A release of the air inside wafted into Power's face. It was cold and smelled musty and earthy. Beyond, there was blackness. He held the lamp up. The room seemed to be so big that the lamp could not illuminate it all. He looked down at the floor beyond. The kitchen tiles stretched out into the gloom. Power knew that the tiles were on stone. The house had been built directly onto the sandstone of the Edge. He still tested the floor beyond with his foot before placing any weight on it. Power also placed a chair in the doorway to prevent the door slamming shut behind him. He had no wish to be trapped. There were no switches anywhere, and presumably the room pre-dated the installation of electricity. The Architect, Alfred Waterhouse, had designed and built the house well before electricity started being used in houses.

The space beyond was a square room with solid stone or brick walls. Sturdy wooden shelves ran round the sidewalls and there was a meat safe on the floor. There were still some tins on the shelves, rusted with age, and some long forgotten Kilner jars containing indistinct bottled fruit from a harvest many decades ago.

'A pantry then' said Power to himself, and breathed a sigh of relief. He felt quite pleased. The space would be useful. But if he used the pantry, where would he put the gargantuan dresser that had covered the entrance.

More confident now, he moved further within the pantry, and then he noticed it.

There was another door at the other end of the pantry.

Power felt his earlier good mood and confidence slip away. There shouldn't be another door.

This door was locked.

Power returned to the kitchen and looked at the debris on the kitchen table, and selected the two rusty keys he had found in the drawers before. He prudently found a can of WD40 and went back to the door and squirted some into the lock. He tried the keys. The first key fitted the keyhole, but didn't fit the lock beyond. The second key fitted the keyhole and the lock. The lock grated in protest, but turned slowly. The key's job done, he took it from the lock. Heart in mouth Power turned the handle and pulled. The door opened into pitch-blackness. Cold air rushed past him. It smelled fresh though. He held the lamp up. There was a small space beyond – a step down to a square platform, carved out of the sandstone. The platform measured maybe a yard square.

Power, again cautiously, propped the door open so that it could not shut behind him and stepped down on to the stone platform.

As he stepped down, he was suddenly aware that there was no wall to his left. Looking to his left, there was nothing but absolute and inky black space. He felt as if he would melt and fall into the blackness. His left arm flailed about and Power gripped the door jamb to steady himself. He felt dizzy and took a moment to orientate himself. He moved his lamp into the void and glimpsed red sandstone steps carved from the Edge itself, disappearing down in to the darkness. He was at a flight of steps leading down into the rock, into the Earth itself.

Power paused and looked back at the warmth and light of the kitchen. What should he do?

Steadying himself with one hand on the wall, he put a tentative footstep down into the darkness onto the first step. He found the step was admirably solid and reassuring and he felt he could venture further. 'Just a little further' he thought. He went down a few steps and the wall made of Waterhouse's brickwork changed to the cool, dry, red sandy rock of the Edge itself. As he went down the stairway, bathed in the luminescent cocoon from the lamp, Power counted. The steps broadened as he went down until he could hold his arms wide apart. He hugged the wall to his left and silently bemoaned the lack of a handrail.

At intervals there were iron loops let into the wall at hand height, as if there once may have been a rope to act as a guide from top to bottom. 'What became of the rope?' Power wondered.

He paused. The steps seemed to be endless. He looked back up at doorway he had come from. It seemed far away and the light leaking from the kitchen was now dim to his eyes. All around was darkness. He heard his own breathing and noted it was both shallow and fast. 'Should I go on?' Power wondered.

He started climbing down again, but more slowly. And then he was at the bottom of the steps. He had counted thirty-eight. 'One short,' he thought. In front of him was a set of two iron gates that stretched across the bottom of the stairs. The gates were affixed to walls, which were ornately decorated with turquoise Victorian tiles. Beyond, stretched an infinity of darkness. Power tentatively pushed at the gates, but they were locked shut. He looked at a thickly rusted chain and padlock that held the two gates shut centrally. He sprayed some more WD40 into the padlock and ferreted in his pocket for the keys to see if one would fit. He rested his hand on the massive iron gates. He exerted only the slightest pressure on the gates as he slotted the key into the padlock. The pressure may have been slight, but it was sufficient to alter the balance of the gates, which had long since rusted through any supports they had on the side walls. For a second the gates balanced and then fell, accelerating towards the stone floor beyond. For a second, Power tried to grip the iron bars as they fell away from him, but his grip was unequal to the sheer weight of the iron. As luck would have it, the iron fell forwards, away from the doctor and his lamp, else he would have been crushed.

The massive iron gates slammed onto the stone floor ahead with a crashing singing noise that reverberated and echoed in a tumult of sound. Power dropped his lamp, swore involuntarily, and clapped his hands to his ears as the ringing sound went on and on.

When at last he opened his eyes and took his hands from his ears, the darkness was silent, but thankfully not total blackness. Miraculously the glass in the lamp had not broken and the light lay at his feet, glowing steadily.

Power picked the lamp up. His hands were shaking and the tremor caused the shadows on the sidewalls to shimmer. He stepped between the fallen gates and moved forward, with great care, looking down at the sandy stone floor. His ears still rang with the noise of the fallen gates, but as they became accustomed to the relative silence Power could now hear the trickling sound of water and occasional sounds of that water dripping from the cave roof. He looked up, but no roof was observable, so high was the cavern.

Power reasoned that the steps had taken him away from the house and that his house, although it stood on solid stone ,was nearby a cave system. He knew that there were caves throughout the Edge, and that they had been used in ancient times as homes for the Mesolithic peoples who hunted on the Cheshire plain hundreds of feet below the Edge. 'Or, it could be a mine', he thought. He knew that Bronze Age people and the Romans had mined for copper and lead, and that later the Victorians had also mined for cobalt there. He walked forward to try and find a wall to see if it had pick marks on it. As he moved forward a drop of water fell on his head. There had been wells in the area, some contaminated by the same ores that others had mined for, such as cobalt. Cobalt was used for blue pottery, and tinting paper. Copper was taken to Macclesfield, combined with calamine from Derbyshire and turned into brass.

He reached out a hand and touched the cavern wall. It was smooth. He couldn't see any pick marks. Maybe this had been a cave where someone had lived thousands of years before. Speculatively, he raised the lamp to the rock to see if there were any paintings. A slow, glistening trickle of water ran down the stone. He shuddered and was cold. The surface was devoid of ornament and bare.

The space around him was some kind of cavern, that was clear, maybe twelve-foot foot high or more, and at least thirty-foot wide. As he explored Power thought it was like an aneurysm, for there were two rounded exits, both narrower. 'Where do they go?' he wondered. From one came faint sounds, maybe voices, or the wind. He asked himself, 'Does this explain the voices I heard? Were there people here the other night, laughing? People living, or ghosts of cave people?'

He ventured closer to one of the tunnels that led away from the space. 'Is this an entrance or an exit', he wondered. He sniffed at the air and thought it fresher, maybe. Did it lead to the surface, and if so, how far did the tunnel run? He had heard there were miles of caves. He had walked some way away from the gates now.

Power had neglected to check how much oil was in the lamp. The light sputtered and went out.

He let out an involuntary cry, which was immediately stifled by the blackness.

Total blackness. No electric light. No candle light. No moon or star light. An absence of light. Utter darkness.

His hearing seemed more acute suddenly. The scrape of the soles of his shoes on the stone floor as he turned about to try and see anything. There was the sound of trickling water here and there. Power could hear the gentle sound of air moving slightly in the cave and loudest of all, the sound of his own breathing, and his own heart beating fast, in fright and panic.

His hands fumbled uselessly at the unseen lamp, and got burned by the still hot metal. 'What am I trying to do?' he asked himself. He remembered the matches, which lay, seemingly a million miles and a million years away, on the kitchen table.

The darkness was permanent. If he waited till day the sun would never penetrate, indeed had never penetrated, here.

He had turned around several times in the last few minutes. Without his sight he had no clue as to his orientation in the cave. If he walked forward would he encounter a rock wall or open space? Was the initial cavern he had entered from the stairway to his left, to his right, forward or back?

"God help me," he whispered. He dropped the lamp and stretched his arms out. The lamp smashed on the floor, the glass tinkling. The lamp uselessly rolled and clattered away.

'Why didn't I take more care?' Power castigated himself. 'Why didn't I wait till I was prepared? Potholers have rope, and torches, and spare batteries, and route maps, and people with them and who know where they are going? Why am I so stupid?' But Power hadn't known the situation he would be facing that night. He had never expected, that last evening, to find a secret stairway. Or else like Ariadne in the Labyrinth, he would have let out a thread to follow back home. Now he was alone, in the dark, with what else? It is easy in the daylight sun to shrug off any fears of the unknown and the supernatural, but alone in the absolute dark, and cold fear grips one's soul absolutely.

Power shouted out, but heard his cry disappearing into space like water disappearing in black sand. The fear in his voice was no comfort.

The open space all around him was disorientating. He walked forward and reached out his hands and touched the walls, planting his palms open wide, feeling the solidity for reassurance that he still existed. He must move. 'Left or right? The answer matters so much,' he thought.

He felt that the air was moving more on his left cheek and wondered if left was the tunnel that led out of the caves. If he moved right would he get to the main cavern, the one that the steps led up from? Or maybe the feeling of air moving was caused by the stairway itself and the open doors to kitchen and the surface? Should he move towards the feeling of moving air or away? He panicked. How and when had he first noticed the feeling of the moving air?

If he got even more lost what would happen? He might move the wrong way, fall down a shaft and break a leg. No one knew he was here. No one would rescue him. No one would find him until it was too late.

He decided. He would move to the right. Inch by inch, feeling his way gradually, testing each and every footstep to avoid any potholes or shafts.

His breathing was rapid and Power felt unable to fight down waves of panic. He felt dizzy and there was a ringing in his ears and his knees felt as if they would give way. He moved his head from left to right, but though his eyes were open he might have been fifty fathoms under the sea. He was suddenly beset by the idea that anything might be watching him and might come at him in the dark.

Power paused, struggling to marshal his composure and breathing. 'I cannot see, but I have all my other senses,' he thought. 'I don't know where the way out is right now, but I do know that there is a way out that I can find'.

Power moved one way along the wall for endless minutes, but he had no way of knowing whether he was getting closer to or further way from his goal. He stopped. The inability to get a drink had made him thirsty and the unavailability of food had made him hungry. His stomach rumbled in the dark and, unexpectedly, he laughed with pleasure on hearing the sound.

Power remembered he had bought a packet of sesame snaps from the hospital shop at lunchtime. The packet had survived the afternoon clinic and now nestled in his jacket. He rummaged in his left hand pocket then his inside breast pocket, but the packet eluded him. Finally, he tried his right hand jacket pocket and there it was. He broke open the pack. The aroma of the sesame seemed so special in the dark. And somehow, the simple taste was magnified into a glory of its own. He snaffled the whole pack in less than a minute.

And then a thought presented itself to him, as from a book he had read a long time ago, 'What have I got in my pocket?' There had been something else in there besides the sesame snaps. He reached again into his right hand pocket and felt something cylindrical, cold and solid. A smile of hope welled up inside him. One of his patients that afternoon had described headaches and double vision. Being conscientious, Power had taken her blood pressure and looked in her eyes to exclude papilloedema. And here in his pocket was the ophthalmoscope he had used in clinic and inadvertently pocketed. Power chuckled. He just hoped that he had switched the ophthalmoscope off after the examination or the battery would be flat. He pulled the scope out of his pocket and switched it. A thin, but bright light shone out like a beacon in the gloom and Power cheered out loud.

He could now see at least a part of the walls and floor. He could see that he was now on the periphery of the first big cavern he had entered. And there, over to his right, was the pair of iron gates lying flat upon the rock in front of him.

Power rushed over to the gates and switched off the ophthalmoscope. He waited while his eyes adjusted and he was able to see the faint light filtering through from the kitchen that would lead him up the steps to home.

He ran up the stairs, two at a time, slamming the door and firmly locking it behind him.

He revelled in the light and warmth of his kitchen and it all began to seem like something of a dream. He wondered about getting the gates re-hung in the next few days and locking them as tightly shut as was humanly possible.

The Soldier
September 1994

"It is actually Real Tennis," said retired Captain Smythe as he showed Dr Power round the court at Blackfriars Road. "Real Tennis was played in the time of Henry V. Henry VIII put courts in all his Royal palaces."

Power looked round the court in some trepidation. He wasn't very sporty and he was a notable failure at tennis and squash. Real Tennis or Royal Tennis seemed to combine the worst aspects of both. There was an indoor tennis court with a net, and the balls could be hit onto the walls around it, making it a fast and unpredictable game. He earnestly wished that he had not accepted Captain Smythe's invitation to 'try the game', but now here he was, dressed to play, standing in the actual court itself and with a racquet in his hand.

There seemed to be no escape.

Captain Smythe was running through the rules and various terms like 'pique', 'chase', 'galleries', 'dedans', 'penthouse', 'yard lines' and so on were running together into a maddening blur in Power's mind. "Perhaps we should have a trial game," suggested Power, "and it might seem clearer?"

Ten exhausting minutes later the game seemed no clearer to him and worse still Power was sweating and breathing hard.

"It's fantastic isn't it?" breezed the Captain enthusiastically.

His opponent had seemingly lost the power of speech to reply. Power wheezed uncomfortably and mused on whether the relatively sedentary life of a psychiatrist could truly be offset by the exercise of an occasional walk on the sandstone Edge and through the fields and hedgerows of rural Cheshire. Nevertheless, Power was determined that he was not about to give up as he began his turn to serve. Although Dr Power's willpower was considerable, it was not enough to compensate for his physical condition. The doctor staggered around the court and his opponent's score was steadily increasing.

It was to Dr Power's great relief that his on-call bleep began to sound and shrilly demand his attention. 'Saved by the bleep,' he thought.

"I'm so sorry," Power said. "I must answer this." He pulled a Nokia 232 mobile phone from his bag at the edge of the court. Power ducked out into the corridor outside the court. He punched the hospital switchboard's number into the phone's keyboard and was swiftly put through to the psychiatric intensive care unit. "Hello, Dr Power here?"

"Dr Power? Are you the on-call consultant tonight? It's Steve here, the charge nurse. I'm sorry to bother you, but there's been an admission. The SHO has seen him, but to be honest, we'd like your opinion. It's an army patient."

"I'll be about forty minutes," said Power. He had never been happier to be called in to the hospital.

He marched back into the tennis court. "So sorry," he said. "I've been called in. An emergency."

Captain Smythe scoffed. "Very convenient, Carl. Very convenient. You need toughening up. You could always join the army, and be a proper doctor . . ."

"I rather thought I was," muttered Dr Power as he collected his things, shook Captain Smythe's hand, said goodbye, and hurried to his ancient car.

Half an hour later Power parked on the road to the hospital and walked past the sentinel-like trees, which lined the avenue that led to the main entrance. Rain dripped from leaves onto the glistening asphalt where Power walked. He ran up the hospital's broad, limestone steps and into the carpeted hall. The hospital receptionist nodded to him, "Good afternoon, Dr Power." She noticed his reddened face. "Have you been running?"

"I've been playing Tennis Royal," said Power as he hurried down the corridor towards the stairs.

The male psychiatric intensive care ward was in the hospital basement, which always troubled Power. 'Why should the most ill patients be hidden away?' he thought. In any case he worried about being underground as if he could sense the weight of the hospital building weighing down on his head. Power unlocked the first airlock door – a Home Office approved seven-lever key was issued to senior consultants – and stepped through into the empty airlock. He carefully locked the door behind him and hurried to the second door. He rang the intercom to let the staff know he was there and to ensure a nurse met him on the other side to keep him safe as he entered the ward corridor. The intercom crackled into life. "Hello," he said. "It's Dr Power."

"We see you," said the nurse in the staff office. Power looked up at the black glass bubble that housed the CCTV camera that monitored the airlock. CCTV cameras covered all areas within the intensive care unit. He nodded to it, wondering whether he was being watched at the moment he did so. "We're a bit busy. Putting your patient into seclusion. Could you be patient for a few moments please, Doctor? There's been an incident."

"What kind of incident?"

"An assault on staff by our new admission. The ambulance has just taken Bobby away." Bobby was one of the older nurses. He liked gardening, Power remembered, and was an amateur DJ who played 1960s soul.

"Is he all right?"

"Broken jaw, we think. Broken arm. Lucky to escape though. He was trying to break Bobby's neck . . . and he has the army training doesn't he?"

"Have you got enough staff?" asked Power. "I'll come in and help."

"We appreciate the offer, but we want to keep you safe Dr Power. Stay there for now please."

Anxious moments followed. Stuck in the airlock, Power could see and hear nothing. He stood between two white steel doors and waited. He looked at the various posters advising relatives that if they wished to visit they must be willing to co-operate with a search. A patient's relative, his own mother, had recently been caught trying to smuggle cocaine into Power's ward in a space inside a mobile phone. Other relatives had tried to smuggle heroin in the base of a tube of crisps. One of the principles of the ward was to create an environment free of street drugs so that men strung out and psychotic on amphetamines and cocaine could detox and hopefully recover. 'Why would someone smuggle something into a ward that would harm their relative,' Power wondered. It didn't make sense, but they did.

Clearly the ward must have been in crisis, but when Carl Power was ushered through the second airlock door and into the fluorescent-lit ICU corridor, all was calm. One or two of his recovering patients nodded and smiled at him as he walked with the nurse to the locked office, which sat by the dining area. The charge nurse who had called Power in, Steve, was sitting in there clasping a mug of tea. He radiated calm professionalism. "Dr Power," he said. "Thank you for coming in. It's been a busy day."

Power looked around the office. It was full of the nursing staff who had just put the new admission in seclusion. They too were sharing a cup of tea and were debriefing. In the corner was Power's trainee, George, who was just a month into his psychiatry job with Power. He looked uncomfortable; shell-shocked. Power made a mental note to speak to George alone and reassure him as soon as was practical.

"Would you like a cup of tea or coffee, Dr Power?" asked Cynthia, the staff nurse. Power nodded and reached over for the mug, then perched on a ward desk and took a sip.

"What's the name of the new admission?" Power asked.

"Private Evans from Wrexham," said Steve. He was brought in from the barracks at Copthorne by six military police. "Private Evans is still a serving officer, just. One of the soldiers of the Royal Shrewsbury Infantry Division, who were in Iraq and liberated Kuwait. And more recently in Bosnia and Croatia. It took six huge armed policemen to get him in here. And as soon as he was through our doors they vanished like smoke."

"Police?" said Power. "What has he done? Or what did they say he had done?"

"Gone AWOL – absent without leave – and when they went to pick him up from his Mum's in Wrexham they found him holed up in his bedroom, with a stack of guns and ammunition under his bed. Two live grenades he's withheld. They said he was 'jabbering' something about some 'People's Army Warlord' he expected to come knocking on his door. Private Evans could have blown his mother's terraced house to bits. He's not a well man . . ."

"And there was an incident on here?" Power looked around the room at the staff. Some looked rather shaky.

"Yes," said Steve. "Bobby was trying to calm Evans down, make him familiar with the ward. Reassure him. You know how experienced Bobby is . . . well, Evans took a dislike and started mentioning that he knew that he's been sent here to be experimented on; castrated, organs removed for transplanting – mentioned this

Warlord he's fixated on. And he just took Bobby to be working for him . . . Evans is a trained killer. He nearly took Bobby's head off. It took six staff to restrain him. We had to call in almost everybody from the other units to contain him."

"What sedation did you prescribe him?" Power looked at George, his trainee.

"I didn't know what to give him . . . I've never seen anyone like that," said George, obviously upset. "His eyes were staring and wide . . . like almost popping out of his head and his neck was bulging and he was just looking into me and his spit was flying everywhere . . . like an animal . . . and he was roaring . . ."

Steve interrupted, "Dr Davis kindly prescribed 6mg of lorazepam and 100mg levomepromazine i.m."

Power nodded, "A substantial dose."

"And it hardly touched the sides," said Steve. "Come and see."

Steve escorted Power out of the office and led him beyond the dining area to the seclusion corridor. Two nurses were sitting outside the seclusion room. Another was watching through an observation window and trying to talk Evans down. Evans was beating against the seclusion room door, which shook and reverberated under his fists. Small trickles of plaster were falling from the ceiling by the seclusion room door. Power thought about what had happened to Bobby and he thought of an SAS man that had been admitted a year or so back who had taken the seclusion room apart from inside, escaped, and scaled the unscalable walls of the exercise yard and absconded over the hospital roof.

"It's impossible to make any kind of detailed assessment of Evans in his current state," said Power. "By rights he should be fast asleep with all that medication. I think . . ." He could hear Steve groaning softly. "We will have to take charge, go in and give him some Acuphase to quiet him. He's too dangerous otherwise. Let him sleep it off overnight and I will see him tomorrow morning, first thing."

"The thought of going in there," said Steve and shook his head.

"And if we don't," said Power, looking up at the flakes of plaster drifting downwards from a small crack that had appeared. "He'll either break his bones or break the door. Summon all the people you can find, and we will go in together."

And in a brief interlude when Evans was sitting down upon his bed, Power led eight nurses into the room and whilst they held Evans arms and legs and head, Power struggled to administer an injection of 150mg, and then after quieting Evans as best they could, they left one by one. Within twenty minutes he was asleep and Power left.

* * *

Power was back on the ward at 9.00 a.m. He had spent an hour earlier in the morning at another hospital visiting Bobby, the nurse who had been attacked. Bobby had been very mournful indeed and announced his intention to retire as soon as he might. Power commiserated with him and encouraged him not to make any decisions too quickly.

On the psychiatric ICU Power found Evans had been transformed overnight. He was being nursed in the seclusion room with the door wide open, as opposed to firmly shut. Two nurses sat near the open door. Evans was munching his way through a mound of bacon sandwiches and swigging on a pint mug of tea.

"All right, Doctor?" Evans greeted Power and stood up, almost to attention.

"Good morning, Private Evans." Power smiled at him around the door jamb. "Did you sleep well?"

"Like a top, Doctor." Although Evans looked dour and did not return Power's friendly smile, he was polite and appropriate.

Power looked at the nurses. They nodded and confirmed that

Evans had slept through the night, and waking settled, they had decided to see how he went on with the door open.

"I'll come back and talk to you later," said Power. "I don't want to disturb your breakfast."

"This is my second plateful, Doctor. You are not interrupting."

For a man who only the previous night had been so disturbed that he needed the heaviest medication, Private Evans was surprisingly calm. Power went to get blank white paper and using his favourite black fountain pen, started to take a medical history.

He chatted with Evans for an hour or so and learned that he had been convinced the night before that the military police were taking him to a medical research centre to be dissected. In the cold light of day he knew that he was now in a true hospital, but he had been convinced last night that his very life was at risk. He had reason. He had been captured in Bosnia and taken to a warlord's lair, where he had been tortured. Most of his lower teeth had been removed with pliers until he talked. Now he talked voluntarily to Power but he trembled, he shook, and occasionally tears sprang to his eyes as he recounted the torture and all the images from the conflict that danced jeeringly in his mind. He told Power of nightmares that slung him from his sleep to find himself in a tangle of bedclothes on the floor, dripping with sweat. And other times when his comrades told him he had been 'somewhere else' and he had been 'back there' in the past, standing in the rain looking at the carnage. He could still summon the feeling of the water running over his scalp and down his neck as he looked at the bodies in the field and then realised that although the guns that had killed them might be silent now, they were also suddenly and stealthily here and pointed at his head. And the uncertain guns had followed him as he was taken to the warlord, Juka. Evans told Power of the rages, triggered by the slightest thing, 'the stupidest thing' and how he drank to forget, and how he would seek out a fight to staunch his blood-red rage. How his wife had left him, for her safety and to his relief, for he didn't like to be touched any more.

Power collected the symptoms and formulated his diagnosis and a management plan, a good one that had a chance of working, given time. He talked to Evans as he did, reassuring him as best he could. "This action, your time in action, is history, part of history and you want to move on, but it keeps clutching at you and clawing you back. We have to stop it. Time will help, but at the same time history is all around us – like cloth draped over everything – clothing us in a many coloured coat we carry with us . . ."

"A blood-coloured coat? Red? Or Black, black blood like the oil we fought over in the Gulf?"

Power stayed silent. He paused, and wrote. In therapy you could say too much and the point of connection, the rhythm and rapport with the patient, would be lost by an ill-judged word.

"Do you think you can manage to stay calm, out on the ward?" Evans nodded. "Well, I will talk to my nursing colleagues and see what they advise. Maybe they can show you your room, but if you feel upset at any time, talk with us." He paused again and looked Evans in the eye. "It will get better. I will see you at the ward round, tomorrow."

And with that Power went to talk to Steve, the charge nurse, and to write up his report.

* * *

Laura had just finished typing up the tape of dictation that Power had given her. Laura was Power's long-serving and equally long suffering secretary. Despite the occasional suffering, she would not change her job or work with any other consultant. Her closer colleagues teased her that she had a crush on him. The morning's work finished, Laura started eating some baked salmon she'd brought to work with her. She was looking forward to a pot of Greek yoghurt and honey, when the phone rang. It was reception. "There's a man on his way to see Dr Power. He's an army officer. I would say officer and gentleman but he's no gentleman. He wouldn't wait down here."

"I'll head him off," said Laura. She put the phone down, and jumped up from her desk in the office next to Power's. She was too late though, for as she hurried into the corridor the abrupt visitor was rapping his knuckles on Dr Power's door. Laura ran her appraising eyes over his stiff iron-grey hair, his dull milky blue eyes and his plum-coloured jacket.

"Excuse me," said Laura, affronted at the visitor's conduct. "Have you got an appointment, please?"

"I don't need one, Miss. The army is paying for a patient at this hospital and the army needs to see the patient's consultant, now."

"Excuse me, I need to know your name, and I need to ask Dr Power whether he will see you." Laura felt an angry blush spreading over her face.

"I am Colonel Arkshaw of the RAMC and who are you, please?"

Laura found it difficult to hold her temper. "I am Dr Power's secretary. Can I ask you to take a seat, please, and I will try and find Dr Power and ask if he can see you."

"Listen, I have a tight schedule. I am the only psychiatrist in the North of England who is able to review this case. There is simply no time to be wasted in this way. I need to see Private Evans and I need to vet Dr Power and see if he's up to the job."

"I'm sorry. Dr Power is a very experienced and senior psychiatrist . . ."

"Is he? Is he? Well, where is he? I'm going down to the ward. Get him to meet me there in half an hour." And with that Colonel

Arkshaw was away down the stairs.

"An officer, but no gentleman . . ." Laura muttered to herself, echoing the receptionist's assessment. She went back into her office and bleeped her consultant. He rang back within five minutes. "Dr Power? The most obnoxious man I have ever met has just turned up and been asking for you."

"Dr Arkshaw?" asked Power.

"Yes," said Laura. "How did you know?"

Power chuckled. "I'm on the ward and he's with poor Private Evans now. I expect he'll get round to me next."

"He is the . . . the . . . rudest man I have ever met," said Laura.

"I will grant you that he does seem a bit opinionated," said Power, smiling.

"It's not funny, Carl. He's a monster. He's trouble."

Power had thought that Arkshaw would be half an hour or so, but within ten minutes of starting his examination of Private Evans, Colonel Arkshaw had finished.

Arkshaw blew into the nursing office, glowering at Dr Power. Steve, the charge nurse, knew an approaching squall when he saw one and signalled subtly to the other nurses that were in the office to leave Dr Power and him alone with Arkshaw. Steve closed the door behind them and receded into the corner of the office, watching the two doctors.

"How long has Evans been here?" demanded Arkshaw.

"Three days I guess. He spent the first night in seclusion and needed Acuphase . . ."

Arkshaw interrupted. "Your diagnosis, Dr Power?"

"Well, we are still assessing Private Evans and . . ."

"Come on! I don't have time for this. I'm the only doctor in the North of England with the power to say whether he's rehabilitated, retired or hoiked out of the army."

"Colonel Arkshaw, I'm sure you'd agree that such a momentous decision about a man's career needs a deal of consideration. We need to keep a close eye on him, observe his behaviour, talk to him about his feelings and symptoms." Arkshaw laughed. Power began to be irritated by the man's plum-coloured jacket.

"You are typical of a civilian psychiatrist. You don't understand and you wouldn't survive in the army of today. This is triage we are after. Is he ill with schizophrenia and retirable? Or has he had a mild wobbler and can be rehabilitated? Or is he a dangerous criminal that has stolen army weapons and needs a spell in jail?"

"It's just too soon to say . . ." said Power.

"Triage, Dr Power. This isn't an academic exercise. What's wrong with him in your august opinion?"

"Well, my working diagnosis is Post Traumatic Stress Disorder."

"How predictable! This is why the army should not have got rid of its psychiatric beds. Military psychiatry should never be in the hands of NHS amateurs. Let me tell you, I don't believe in PTSD. It doesn't exist! It's all alcohol. The average squaddie can sink more alcohol in a week than you can drink in a year. And the alcohol makes them develop anxiety disorders . . . like stage fright. Detox them and they are good to go back into service."

At some point in the conversation Power's jaw had dropped open. He was struggling to assimilate what he had just heard. "But . . . but surely it's not a matter of faith," said Power. "PTSD exists. It's a recognised medical disorder. And Private Evans has nightmares, flashbacks, irritability, re-living experiences . . ."

"And all of those symptoms can be produced by alcohol dependence or faked."

Steve stepped in, "Private Evans is genuinely ill, sir."

It was as if Colonel Arkshaw was unaware of Steve or his having said anything. He betrayed no sign of having heard him.

"Dr Power, I came here to see if your unit was up to looking after military personnel. I'm having my doubts. I've examined Evans . . ."

"For only about ten minutes!" Power was losing his temper now.

"I have examined him," said Arkshaw. "He is an alcoholic. His drinking is notorious."

Power protested. "We've taken blood tests for liver function and drugs and we've tested his urine for drugs and . . ." Steve laid a hand on Dr Power's arm. Power looked at him questioningly. Steve shook his head, willing Power not to argue further.

"When will your report be ready, Dr Power?" asked Arkshaw.

"I've dictated a draft report, but I wouldn't dream of releasing it this early, it's just preliminary."

"Can your secretary let me have a copy as soon as possible, Dr Power? I need to write the official report tomorrow and it will be a source. I expect your report to follow my views, of course."

And with that, Colonel Arkshaw turned on his heel and marched to the airlock. He ordered a nurse to let him out, and was gone.

Steve saw that Power was shaking with anger. "Cup of tea, Dr Power?" he started pouring boiling water on some teabags in mugs. "I'm sorry I interrupted, but I thought that Colonel Arkshaw was a bit of a closed book." He had been worried that the confrontation would escalate, to no avail.

"Laura did warn me," said Power, sitting down with his steaming mug of tea. "You are right, Steve, he wasn't here to listen."

"Well, he certainly wasn't going to get a cup of tea from me."

* * *

Power's report had been written, signed, and faxed to the Ministry. Laura noted with satisfaction that Power had not amended it in any way after his encounter with 'the most obnoxious doctor in Christendom' as Power had called Arkshaw. Power had stuck to his diagnosis of PTSD and over the course of the next few days he had observed an improvement in Evans, who took his medication, engaged in therapy from the psychologist, and repeatedly apologized for his attack on Bobby, the nurse Evans had encountered on admission. "I wasn't thinking straight, I thought he was someone else . . . I'm so sorry." He offered to personally apologise to Bobby. Power didn't think it was the time.

First thing on a Friday morning, whilst Power was at another hospital, Laura took a call from Steve on the intensive care unit. "Is Carl there?" She explained where he was. "I need to speak with him, when he gets back. The MPs arrived at six a.m. this morning."

"MPs?" Laura didn't quite understand what Steve meant.

"The Military Police, Laura, not a bunch of politicians."

"All right. I get you now. What for?"

"To take Private Evans away. They had the paperwork. There was nothing to be done, but Carl's patient has gone. I wanted to let him know. He'll be upset."

"Where did they take Private Evans?"

Steve consulted the ward diary, a chaotic biro-ed repository of such information. "Somewhere in Colchester. They said it was a correctional facility. I did protest that Evans was ill and a patient. But they said that Dr Plum had graded him as a criminal, not a patient."

"Dr Plum?"

"That dreadful bloke in the plum-coloured smoking jacket thing."

"How could I forget?" said Laura.

"And you know Dr Power's report?"

"I typed it."

"I read the file copy," said Steve.

"Well?"

"Carl won't like Dr Plum's official report. The MPs left a copy with the ward. Dr Arkshaw deliberately changes Carl's findings. He misquotes Carl. This is what Dr Arkshaw says," Steve began to read the report out over the phone, "'Dr Power has kindly prepared a report which specifically rules out the possibility of PTSD and raises the question of Evan's psychopathy. My examination of Evans concurs with Dr Power's and I can find no evidence of mental illness. Evans is fit to stand trial for theft of weaponry, ammunition and absence without leave.' And when I protested to the MPs, as they were on their way out of the door with Evans, they said it was none of a civilian's business and that we'd better keep out of it if we knew what was good for us."

"You're right," said Laura. "Carl won't be happy at all."

"I don't think there's much he can do though. They were a bit threatening. And to change what Dr Power said in his report . . ."

"No. He won't like that. And if I know Dr Power, he certainly won't leave it there."

The Scissors
September 1994

The red-brick cottage was small and well-kept. The lawns were as neat, smooth and short as green velvet. Purple clouds of wisteria hung around the eaves of the cottage and bees still buzzed their frantic way about the flowers. Summer was loathe to die and Autumn was lazily late. The shrubs had been most precisely shaped by a well-practiced hand. White Agapanthus sat alongside blue Plumbago and red Salvia. The borders were scrupulously free of weeds. The cottage itself had freshly painted window frames, with shimmering clean glass and a shiny red front door.

Dr Power looked at the cottage in wonder and admiration as he sat inside his shabby Saab. He was waiting patiently, parked across the road, in the sleepy village of Antrobus, Cheshire.

The tranquil scene did not reflect the panicked phone call his secretary Laura had received from Michael Eddy's family doctor. According to the GP, Michael had attended the surgery 'ranting' about how evil his father was and how his father kept him up all night, 'whispering prayers to Satan' in his bedroom next door.

The community nurse records had showed that Michael had only one missed depot injection, but he was known to dabble in other substances; cannabis, amphetamines and sometimes Michael would even smoke sage (through water) from his father's herb garden.

Father and son had lived together ever since his mother had died of an embolism four years earlier. The father was devoted to his son and lavished as much care and attention to his son's welfare as he did his immaculate cottage. Mr Eddy senior was fiercely protective of his son.

Power had no answer to his knocking at both front and back doors. He had noticed that there was no car in the cottage's drive, and could have easily assumed that both Mr Eddy and his son were out. However, Power had been sure that he saw the bedroom curtains upstairs twitch ever so slightly, swing from side to side and fall back still.

Power had decided that the son was possibly inside the cottage, but not answering the door, and that he might wait for a little while longer to see if Mr Eddy returned. Power completed the day's crossword in *The Guardian*.

Power was just beginning to think he would be better deployed back at the hospital, when Mr Eddy drove his polished Volkswagen into the cottage's driveway. He was alone. Power watched Mr Eddy getting bags of shopping out of the hatchback and waited for him to lock the car up before getting out of his own. Power carried his on-call bag with him. Inside were sets of notes, plain white paper, pens and a small supply of prescription drugs, both tablets and injections.

Power hailed his patient's father, "Hello, Mr Eddy?"

Mr Eddy turned to regard Dr Power from under a shock of white hair, with his pale blue eyes. Mr Eddy was shorter than Power, and stocky. He wore a check shirt with sleeves rolled up showing stout forearms, which were grizzled with grey hair. He stood stiffly, as if at attention, and his beige Farah trousers had exquisitely sharp vertical creases. By contrast Power's Saab looked shabby and in need of a good wash to Mr Eddy. Power himself was clean, but looked as if he could have spent more time on ironing his clothes, which were evidently chosen for comfort and practicality rather than to impress anyone from the older generation. The 'Appearance' of a patient was one of the first things that Power taught his students to examine, and yet it was remarkable how little time he spent in cultivating his own appearance.

One thing, however, was amiss with Mr Eddy's face. His right eye was blackened. Mr Eddy did not strike Power as the village brawler, and Power made a mental note to determine how Mr Eddy had been injured so.

"I'm Dr Power, your son's Consultant."

"I know," said Mr Eddy, and his body language said that he wanted to get into the cottage as soon as possible. He looked warily over his shoulder at the cottage windows.

"His GP asked me to call and see him. That would be all right wouldn't it?"

"Er . . . I'm not sure he's in. Maybe it would be better if you came back?" Mr Eddy quailed under Dr Power's steady gaze, was not a good liar and he could see that Power saw through him.

"I think I could help you both," said Power. "If you let me in that is?"

"Maybe," said Mr Eddy, "but please don't say anything that would upset Michael, or make him think that I'd called you?"

"Michael went to the GP himself and the GP was worried for you, for both of you."

"Okay, but please be as discreet as you can be? I have to live with Michael after you lot go . . ."

As they went in, Michael was sitting on the stairs opposite the front door. He glared at his father and then turned his stare onto Power. "You let him in," he growled at his father.

"Be polite. We're polite to visitors Michael, aren't we?"

"Would you like a cup of tea, Dr Power?" said Michael in a sing song voice through a fake smile.

"Can you give me a hand with the bags please, son?" Mr Eddy said. "Let's take them through to the kitchen. Dr Power, will you take a seat in the parlour? I'll make us some coffee."

"Oh, it's all right," said Power. "I'm fine."

Power entered the parlour. He guessed that the décor had been kept exactly the way it was when Mrs Eddy had been alive. There was a preponderance of chintz. There was a coffee table though and this was covered in pages cut out of the New and Old Testaments. In places the text was heavily underlined. He picked one up at random. It was Exodus 22.8. An ashtray was so overflowing with cigarette butts that they spilled over onto the cottage rugs that covered the red tile floor.

Power could hear voices raised in disagreement from the kitchen down the passageway. At length, Mr Eddy brought in a tray of coffee, which he set down on the table, obscuring the dissected Bible. Power particularly hadn't wanted any hot drinks. He smiled though and made sure he poured cold milk in his mug. He watched as the father did the same. By now Michael was sitting in the prime chair by the fire-place. "I'm going to take my coffee into the kitchen," said Mr Eddy. "And leave you in peace to talk to Michael." Michael glared at Dr Power as his father edged out of the parlour.

"I've to talk to you, he says."

"Thank you," said Power. "You went to see your GP?"

"I did."

"That's why I have been asked to see you, Okay?

"Yes, Okay. You've seen me now."

"Can we talk a bit?"

"Dad doesn't want me to."

Power was surprised by this. "Why not?"

"You're trying to trick me, Dad said you would."

The doctor shook his head. "I'm just trying to find out how you are. Your GP was worried you weren't sleeping. Are you sleeping okay, Michael?"

"No. He's up all night. Keeping me awake. Chanting or something in his room."

"Your Dad?" Power tried as best as he could to keep any incredulity out of his voice.

Michael nodded. "He's not what he seems. He is praying to Satan at midnight. The witching hour. He controls a coven in the village."

"Do you see him praying or chanting? Or just hear him through the walls?"

"When I go into his room he's in the dark; pretending to be asleep. We argued a couple of days ago. He said I woke him up and he shouted that I could have given him a heart attack. We fought."

Power nodded. "What if he was asleep, Michael? What if these prayers were just . . . voices?"

"No, no," said Michael, absolutely convinced that he was right.

"Did you hit your Dad? I can see he's sporting a good old black eye. Did you thump him?"

"He fell in the dark."

"You said that the prayers you hear are your Dad in the room next door. Do you ever hear anything else out of the ordinary?"

"I hear angels. They tell me that you cannot live in the same place as a Satanist. That my Dad and I can't be here together."

"Your Dad would miss you, I guess. You're all he's got now," said Power.

"His mind is on other things," said Michael, through gritted teeth. "On the devil's work."

Power decided to challenge the delusion. "Surely not, Michael. Wasn't he a church warden once? I think that I remember that he told me at a clinic appointment you had."

"He **was** a church warden when Mum was alive. When she died he no longer had to pretend he believed in God."

Power pointed to the scattered pages from the Bible on the table.

"Did you cut the pages out Michael?"

Michael nodded. "I've pasted pages and pages of the Bible on my wall. On the wall that separates his room from mine. The Holy Word will keep his prayers from harming me."

"I'm sure he wouldn't want to harm you," said Power.

Suddenly Michael's face was an inch away from Power's. Power could smell the tobacco on Michael's stale breath. "What would you know, heathen man?" Michael sat back just as abruptly. Power watched his agitated nicotine yellowed fingers tapping on the arm of the chair.

"Have you stopped your medication?"

"Weeks ago, the devil controls the chemists. I could see the microscopic structure of the molecules of the drugs as they coursed through my veins. Each molecule had been engineered to be an upside down cross. Evil. Pure chemical evil."

"The angels. What else do they say? Do they tell you to do things?"

"They keep me safe. Tell me when to eat, when to sleep. Tell me who I should have kept out of the house." He glared at Power and the doctor was uncomfortably afraid that violence was imminent.

"Would you like me to go, Michael?" Michael nodded.

"I will just say goodbye to your Dad," Power stood up and was about to leave the room when he thought he would chance one final question. "Would you consider coming into hospital? For a few days – so we can get your medicine sorted out?" The answer was no. Michael shook his head, slowly and determinedly.

Power found Mr Eddy sitting at a deal table in the kitchen. He was munching a ham and pickle sandwich. A pint mug of tea sat by his plate. Mr Eddy nodded to Power. There were tears in his eyes. "You want him to go into hospital, I guess."

"Yes," said Power. "He has relapsed, but you will know that yourself. I gather you and he had a fight?"

"He came into my room, shouting about the devil. I was sound asleep and being so suddenly awoken . . . I was disorientated. I lashed out. He lashed back." He pointed to his eye. "Hence the shiner."

"He needs to restart his medication, Mr Eddy."

"He could take his tablets here. I don't want him to go away again."

"But . . . until he's stabilised on the antipsychotics again . . . there's a risk to you, Mr Eddy. A real risk."

"I'm his father, Dr Power. I signed up for this. I will accept any consequences."

Power thought for a moment and balanced the facts of the case with his intuition. "You and I both know the risk. He's not in charge of his actions, the illness is. He has all sorts of ideas about you and hears you chanting to the devil. I am worried for you. I know you are happy to accept that risk, but can I leave you alone with him? Let's try something." He reached into his on-call bag and removed a blister pack of olanzapine. "Try giving him one of these now. You try him with a tablet and a glass of water. Please?"

Mr Eddy agreed and left the room with a glass of tap water and one of Power's tablets. He came back in five minutes, shaking his head. "He says he won't take it and that you might be a poisoner."

"That's a pity," said Dr Power. "I think I need to arrange things, Mr Eddy. Arrange an admission. I'm sorry about this, but things won't get any better unless we intervene." Mr Eddy slumped visibly. "I'm sorry." He gave Mr Eddy his card. "I am going back to the hospital now and someone from my team will be in touch this afternoon. Please can you and Michael stay here for them to speak to? Please phone me if you have any problems."

* * *

The call came through on his mobile that evening when Power was eating a home-made chilli and drinking a frosted glass of *Pacifico Clara*.

"Dr Power?"

"Speaking," he said, trying to speak through a mouthful. His forehead was streaming with perspiration and he wondered if he'd cut up too many green chillis.

"Margaret Lindow here. Duty approved social worker. You called me out to see a Mr Michael Eddy. I've been to the cottage and I'm informing you of my assessment."

"Thank you for seeing him," said Dr Power. "Did you complete the paper work for his admission?"

"I did not."

Power spluttered a fine spray of chilli over his kitchen table. The droplets looked like an attack of rust on the table top. "I'm sorry, I think I misheard that?"

"I don't think you did," she said humourlessly.

"But he's floridly psychotic and he's a danger to his father. He needs to come in and be treated on a Section 3."

"I did read your assessment, Dr Power. Would you be so kind as to listen to mine?"

"Go ahead," said Power wiping both his forehead and mouth with a napkin. "Enlighten me."

"Well, Dr Power, we social workers are not mere handmaidens to the doctor, just here to rubberstamp things. We have our own statutory duties. Which we take very seriously." Power sat back in his chair and closed his eyes to endure the lecture. "I have seen Mr Eddy, and you are correct. He is not sleeping well. He has some unusual ideas I grant you, but everything has its context." Power swallowed the temptation to argue. "He denies any desire to hurt his father though. His father also does not want him to go into hospital and opposes any admission. As you know, for a section 3 we do require the Next of Kin's agreement. And that is why I have not completed the Section papers."

"But I think that the father is at risk. The GP also thinks the father is at risk and that was why he asked me to visit."

"Yes, I know that you two doctors have made your medical recommendations, but as you know there are safeguards to protect people against the misuse of the Act, and that is why we have the approved social worker."

"With the greatest respect, you could displace the nearest relative – that would be a technical way round the problem – and then we could still admit Michael. His father is in a difficult position – haven't you taken that into consideration. He's got to live with Michael afterwards so he wouldn't want to spoil his relationship. He doesn't want to be parted from Michael either. Despite all of that he is still at risk. You could displace him."

"As you well know, Dr Power, I didn't write the Act or the Code of Practice. I can't change them for you. Now then, I've phoned you and I've discharged my duty. Good night."

* * *

Power woke at 5 .15 a.m. precisely. Whenever he was worried he woke early. He showered and breakfasted at 6.30 a.m. and was on the road by 7.30 a.m. He was drawing into the village of Antrobus by 8.15 a.m.

Power climbed out of his car with his medical on-call bag clutched in his grasp. He knocked on Mr Eddy's door and waited in the hope that he would answer quickly and allay Power's fears. However, Mr Eddy did not answer and Power could see that his car was still in the driveway.

The doctor moved from the front door to the windows. He could not see anyone within, but as he moved around the cottage he noted an overturned coffee table in the living room, with Bible pages strewn everywhere, and a kitchen scattered with broken crockery and glass. And his anxiety grew.

Power found him on the rear lawn, half hidden behind a shrub. He glimpsed the old man's legs first. One slipper on, one slipper off, and striped pyjamas. The skin of his legs was white, like marble, against the bedewed grass. His eyes were open and staring at the sky moving above his head. There was a patch of brown by his head on the manicured green turf. A pool of blood had run over the grass and sunk into the earth. By the left side of Mr Eddy's head were the silver handles of a large pair of scissors. The blades were sunk deep into Mr Eddy's shoulder. Mr Eddy's dressing gown was soaked with blood. "Oh no, oh no," murmured Power as he sank to his knees beside the body. The wetness of the lawn seeped into his knees. Power put his medical bag down and opened it, just in case. He felt for a pulse at Eddy's wrist and could find none. He pressed as gently as he could over the right carotid artery. To Power's great surprise there was a very weak and thready pulse. Life still resided in Mr Eddy. To underline this fact Power noticed Eddy's eyes drift slowly over to look at him. "Don't move," said Power. "We need to get help." Mr Eddy appeared to be trying to whisper something, but Power hushed him.

Power felt in his pocket for his phone and opened it. There was a signal; it was as weak as the pulse in Mr Eddy's arteries, but present. Power summoned an ambulance and requested a trauma surgeon attend as well. He begged them to be quick. Power had wondered whether to attempt a removal of the scissors himself, but thought that he would leave the decision to more enlightened surgical hands. He tried to remember the name of the thin branch of the subclavian artery that must have been cut by the blades. It must have been a thin thread off the main artery. He reasoned that in amateur hands like his withdrawing the scissors would raise the risk of severing the larger artery. Power took off his jacket and covered Mr Eddy to try and warm him. He thought he should perhaps get some blankets from inside the house.

He noticed then that Mr Eddy was trying to say something again and tried to shush him, but the old man's eyes seemed full of alarm so he leant close to try and hear the pantomime whisper that escaped from the old man's lips.

"Behind you," he said.

Time seemed to slow. Power turned and, seeing Michael wielding a long plank of wood above his head, jumped backwards in a reflex movement. He fell back against the shrub and crashed through it. He raised a leg to try and fend off the blow. The blow fell heavily against his sole, and his leg crumpled backwards, his thigh landing against his midriff. Power stared at the plank, now hovering a few inches from his head. Michael had driven two six inch nails through the head of the plank, and the wickedly sharp points were inches from his face. The nails had been intended to pierce Power's skull and murder his keen brain. With all his might Power kicked upwards against the plank, throwing Michael off balance. Michael fell backwards, away from his father, by the side of Power's medical bag. Power knew any advantage he had would be fleeting. He threw himself at Michael's body and tried to pin him down. Michael wriggled and bucked under Power's weight. Power was worried that he would not be able to hold Michael. Michael made a tactical mistake and somehow rolled round underneath Power's weight – onto his front. Power tried a question to distract his opponent, "Why did you stab your Dad?" Power reached over to the medical bag he had brought. There was a syringe that Power had pre-loaded with 6mg of lorazepam. He pushed it without warning into Michael's deltoid muscle and squeezed the plunger in. Michael shouted out, tried to throw Power off. Power was ready for the sudden movement and he repeated his question. "Why did you stab your Dad?"

"Evil . . ." gasped Michael. "He's evil. Like you. Like you. The spirit of Atropos told me to end his fate with shears. He ran out here, but he wasn't fast . . . enough." He was finding it difficult to breathe. Power knew it was dangerous to try and restrain someone face down, but he had little choice on his own and precious little chance of success unless the medication started to work soon.

Power fumbled in his bag for a 100mg syringe of Acuphase. Slower acting, but longer lasting. This too he administered to Michael's rage. Again the needle provoked him to buck under Power, but Power anticipated the timing again and succeeded in the restraint.

There was no more that Power could do, and he was frightened that he would not be able to hold Michael until the sedation worked. If his strength failed and Michael struggled free he would continue his violence, perhaps kill both Power and his desperately weak father.

Michael, however, had stopped struggling and was beginning to snore. The medication had started to work sooner than Power had thought it would. Power could hear the distant sirens of the emergency services and shaking with the after effects of adrenaline, he sighed in relief.

The Porsche
October 1994

Dr Power stood across the road and surveyed a scene of utter devastation. He was not alone. A small crowd of people stood with him and he could hear them muttering and gossiping. The police were holding the inquisitive crowd at bay and there was even a line of tape that cordoned off the garage and its forecourt. Nearby stood an ambulance, ready to take people to the hospital. The paramedics were inside. A fire engine was also parked nearby and two fire officers stood assembling a Venturi proportioner and foam making branchpipe. There was a smell of petrol in the air. Gathering his courage Dr Power began to walk across the road, and in doing so, accomplished a transition from being amongst the grumbling crowd and relative immunity from gossip, to a protagonist in the drama that was being played out. As he strode across the tarmac to the other pavement he moved from being spectator to participant.

A police officer moved to intercept him and Power explained who he was and showed his NHS identity card. The police officer lifted the tape up so Power could enter the scene.

There were black skid marks on the pavement indicating that there may have been some use of the brakes. As he walked much closer to the car showroom though, there was a crunching underfoot. Small cubes of glass had exploded from the plate glass windows and seemingly the small green cubes had landed everywhere.

At the threshold of the showroom the glass had tumbled down into an opaque triangular prism of glass fragments. Power stepped over it as best he could.

Power could not take his eyes off the cars. Unlike a normal car showroom this was not a world of obsessional order, pristine leather and gleaming paintwork. This was car carnage.

A brand new red Porsche 968 had been driven at speed into the front of the garage, through the polished plate glass, and now sat atop two other new cars, another 968 and a Carrera. All three had been simultaneously transformed in a tiny fragment of time from expensive objects of consumer desire to worthless wrecks.

Only three people, besides the emergency services, remained to be evacuated from the petrol-soaked ruined building. The emergency services were eager to leave, and glad to see the doctor.

The garage owner, Simon Clark, was standing by a senior police officer, discussing matters in an animated fashion. He wished to press charges for the damage. Sitting glumly nearby was the salesman, Mr Ormerod. Mr Ormerod had been a passenger in the Porsche as it hurtled through the window on its airborne path back into the showroom. He now wore a neck collar and was having his blood pressure taken by two paramedics. Mr Ormerod felt unwell and looked downcast. The owner's vitriolic rebukes had left him wondering whether he still had a job. On the whole, he rather thought that he did not. He looked around the wreckage that surrounded him and wondered about jobs he could apply for. The thought of making a claim occurred to Mr Ormerod and he began to groan in simulated pain to the paramedics.

The third person was sitting on a banquette. His right wrist was handcuffed to the left wrist of a police constable. The PC was a tall and burly man, but he was dwarfed by the leonine bulk of Mr Rubici Hammadi. He was both broader and taller than the PC and with long curly dark hair and brown eyes looked like a monstrous mountain beside the policeman. Power could see, even at a distance, that he was agitated and laughing. The policeman was not smiling and his expression was apprehensive. Spotting the doctor, Rubici stood up, necessarily dragging the police officer with him. "Sit down, sir." hissed the officer. Rubici either did not hear him or decided not to listen. Rubici held his arms up in generous welcome to Dr Power. The police constable dangled bodily from Rubici's arm. "SIT DOWN," he shouted.

"My doctor!" Hammadi boomed, and grinned broadly. Technically, Power was not Mr Hammadi's consultant, but Power had previously looked after Hammadi while his colleague was away on leave.

"Rubici," said Power quietly. "Maybe you can sit down? We can talk." Power pointed at the bench.

Hammadi dropped his backside back onto the bench and the police constable staggered to rest beside him.

Power introduced himself the police constable, "I'm Dr Power, a consultant psychiatrist. I've been asked to come and see Mr Hammadi. I have met him before." Power looked at the handcuffs. "Are those needed? I don't think Mr Hammadi will run off, will you Rubici?"

"I promise, doctor."

Mainly to avoid further trauma to his own wrist the PC unlocked the cuffs and sat forlornly rubbing the reddened skin. Rubici laughed to be free and began to gabble, excitedly. "Free as a bird . . . to fly . . . how we flew Dr Power! Flying power, flower power, self raising flour power!" He stood up and began pacing and as he did so he mimed the trajectory the Porsche 968 had taken. "Whoosh! Whoosh! Just like that! We hit the kerb and FLEW!"

"You were driving?" asked Power.

Rubici corrected him. "I was the pilot, Dr Power. We flew – albeit at low altitude, I grant you, but we flew."

"And crash landed," observed the doctor, gazing at the red 986 that sat atop the mangled remains of two other cars.

"Crash smash, no cash!" Hammadi's thoughts were flying too.

Power knew that Rubici suffered with bipolar disorder and it was a short step to the diagnosis of mania. Power wondered how on earth Hammadi had convinced Mr Ormerod that he was well enough to take a test drive.

"Look at the cars, Rubici, and the window, what were you thinking? Are you taking your medicines – whatever medicines Dr Jones has prescribed?"

"Lithium," snorted Hammadi dismissively. "It tastes of metal. It colours my food and does not keep me on my mettle."

"It keeps you well. You could have been killed. Your passenger, the salesman, could have been killed, or a pedestrian." Power wondered how far he could go with the remonstration. Hammadi was beginning to look irritable.

"I can pay for it all. I brought my cheque book, look. I bought the car before we took it on the road. I am an honest man, Dr Power. I can buy the other two and repair the window." He reached out and squeezed Power's cheek enthusiastically. It hurt, but Power said nothing, judging that there was only a fine line between Hammadi's apparent joviality and a blazing temper. Power knew full well that there was probably nothing in Hammadi's bank account. Rubici's private treatment from Dr Jones was funded by his brother.

"He signed the order form," said Mr Ormerod, who had been listening. It wasn't difficult to overhear Rubici's conversation, which was at a stentorian level. "I had the cheque. I thought I was just familiarizing Mr Hammadi with his new car."

"It flew!" Hammadi stood up excitedly again, miming the flight.

"You should have waited for cleared funds. It's policy!" The owner said to Mr Ormerod, joining in the discussion. His objection threatened to turn the conversation into an argument.

"Maybe that can all be sorted out later?" suggested Power.

The garage owner glared at Power as if he too was responsible for Hammadi's actions. Power knew that no court would accept the contract as valid.

Hammadi, a cultured man, was now declaiming Shakespeare at high volume, "For bounty, that makes gods, does still mar men. My dearest Lord, bless'd, to be most accursed, Rich, only to be wretched, thy great fortunes Are made thy chief afflictions."

And as Hammadi quoted the Bard he moved around the twisted metal of the three Porsches, appraising the whole. "An installation, call the Tate. I shall call it My Crush on a Car Crash."

Power looked in his on-call bag to check whether he had packed the right drugs. He stood up and joined Hammadi as he finished his circuit round the cars.

"What now Rubici? I think maybe it's time to have some medicine? Maybe come into hospital again?" Hammadi's mood appeared to have dipped somewhat and for a brief instant, insight was pricking the bubble of his mania. He surveyed the destruction his illness had driven him to.

"What have I done, Dr Power? It seemed such a bright, light day this morning, when everything was possible; everything was infinity about me. It was an expanding universe. My liquid being travelled outward as far as it would go!" His eyes shone.

"How's your sleep?"

His thoughts were speeding up again. "No timetosleep Doctor. Toomanythoughtstoomuch to do. Maybe I should inventtheflyingcar? Whatdoyouthink?"

"Maybe some rest first? I have something to help in my bag – would you take it?"

"Not haloperidol please . . . it does the jaw thing . . . raw, jaw, roar."

"Let's try something else then, I have some Clopixol in my bag. I can give you some of that and then we can take you to hospital."

"Your ward, Dr Power? Your care?"

"Is that what you'd like?"

Hammadi nodded.

Power took Hammadi into an office and administered the injection. Hammadi muttered to himself, soberly. Power patted Hammadi's shoulder and led him out to the bench outside. The police were asking everybody to move out of the showroom so the fire brigade could make all safe. There was still some risk of fire from the fuel. Power negotiated with the paramedics to take Rubici to his own hospital and not Dr Jones' private ward. Under the influence of the sedative Hammadi's mood seemed to be dipping downwards and some insight was surfacing.

"I'm sorry," he said. I didn't want to take Dr Jones' tablets because of the side effects. So I stopped. And then my mood lifted, went upwards like a bird, and so by then I felt I didn't need any medication at all. I didn't mean to . . ." He looked around the chaos of the showroom. "Oh dear . . . what have I done?"

The Shooting Range
December 1994

"I shouldn't be refreshing your training, Andrew, let alone training your friend. Weapons are only to be issued to specifically appointed officers in the Armed Response Unit. There's no need to, or point in, training ordinary officers like yourself," said Inspector Daevid Alleyn. Alleyn was Head of the Armed Response Team and looked after both police firearms and dog units.

"He's had a difficult time, he needs to have his confidence boosted. He's one of the Chief Constable's special advisers. Helped us with both the Ley Man case and also the arson at Heaton Hall. A huge help to the force. We nearly sent the wrong person down for the arson. And he's been attacked twice in the line of duty. This would give him some confidence."

"And he's not a police professional Andrew. He's a professional psychiatrist as you know, and here you are doing your amateur psychiatry on him. He won't thank you for it, quite frankly. And if he is upset by these two incidents, then why on earth would you put a gun in his hands. Who has ever heard of an armed psychiatrist, for Christ's sake?" There was a pause and silence at the end of the line. Alleyn realised that he had perhaps offended Lynch's religious sensibilities. "Oh, I'm sorry Andrew. Didn't mean anything by that."

"Apology accepted. I am not talking about arming Dr Power. Just giving him some confidence. In case he ever gets into some situation where he needs to use something to defend himself maybe. And he is probably more sane than any police colleague I've ever met, and you arm police officers."

Alleyn had thrown himself off balance by blaspheming down the phone at the famously religious Superintendent Lynch. "Oh maybe, we've got some down time on Friday afternoon if that's any good? We finish the training programme and break for Christmas."

"And you can come round for supper at mine afterwards, if you like," offered Lynch. Lynch could hear Alleyn considering the prospect.

"Might there be one of your wife's steak pies?"

"There might be pie, yes," said Lynch. "And a few bottles of Belgian beer."

"Well, all right then." The deal was done.

Lynch grinned. "What time?"

"2.30 in the afternoon," said Alleyn.

* * *

Dr Carl Power was unaware of such trades, or that his friend Superintendent Lynch intended to take him to the Cheshire Police firing range that afternoon. He merely knew that Laura had put 'Advising Cheshire Police' in his diary for Friday afternoon.

Lynch picked him up from the hospital main entrance – a classical sandstone portico with Ionic Columns and pediment. Power was standing in the chill greyness of the December afternoon. Lynch's Audi swept round the turning circle in front of the main doors and Power got in.

"Hello Andrew," he said, as he put on his seatbelt and settled into the modern comfort of Lynch's car – it was a very different vehicle to Power's battered old Saab. Lynch's car was sleek, scrupulously well-maintained and tidy inside. "What's this all about?"

"We're off to the police armoury and training range," said Lynch as his car purred out of the hospital grounds and onto the hedge-lined lanes that cut through the Cheshire countryside. The winter hawthorn hedges were scraggy. "We're going to get some practice."

"What?" exclaimed Power. "Whatever for?"

"Defence," said Lynch. "I don't revel in such things, but a knowledge of weaponry is essential to defend yourself and others who depend upon you for protection."

"You do surprise me," said Power somewhat absently as he stared out of the side window at the green fields whizzing past. For a moment his eye was drawn to a bird of prey, a buzzard, hovering over a field, ready to swoop down. "I thought you were a man of peace. A Biblical Christian soul . . ." As he watched, the buzzard dived and he lost sight of it beyond a thicket of thorns.

Lynch smiled. "I'm not a berserker."

"But guns," said Power. "They're not my style, and I certainly wouldn't think that a Christian would have anything to do with them."

"Those who live by the sword, die by the sword and all that?"

"Exactly," said Power. "That's Biblical isn't it?"

"Matthew 26, I believe," said Lynch. "But I think it's a matter of emphasis. I think few religions condone wanton violence – 'living by the sword', but even Jesus' disciples thought it wise and justifiable to carry a few swords for defence. That's in Luke if you want to check up."

The Weapons Unit was based near Winsford. Precisely on time for their appointment Lynch's Audi purred to a halt outside.

Alleyn was pacing up and down in the entrance hall of the building. Power instantly noticed his frown and apparent agitation. Nearby, a rather mournful looking Sergeant Beresford was sitting on a plastic couch. "Andrew!" barked Alleyn as Lynch advanced upon him; Lynch's right hand was outstretched to shake his hand. "We've been joined by your colleague, Sergeant Beresford. Am I training the whole of your team now?"

"Ah, Daevid, I knew you wouldn't mind."

From the body language of Alleyn and Beresford, Dr Power could see that there was no doubt that Alleyn did mind and had clearly expressed something of the sort to the rather dejected Sergeant Beresford. "Oh, if there's any difficulty I'm quite happy to sit this one out," Power offered. "I guess that Sergeant Beresford needs weapons training far more than I do."

"Now we are here, Carl, there is no backing out. I know what you are like . . . and what you are about," Power groaned inwardly. "I'm sure one more won't make that much difference, will it Daevid?"

"I suppose not," said Alleyn grudgingly. "Come on, let's make a start then. I'll get the signing-in book." Alleyn went off to get the book and a pen.

Whilst he was gone, Power turned to Lynch. "Is Inspector Alleyn always this stressed?"

"Always," said Lynch. "He can be jollied along though."

"He was really grumpy when I rolled up," said Beresford. "Seems to see all firearms as beyond us mere mortals. All a bit elitist if you ask me."

"But you wouldn't like all police to be armed, like in the States, would you?" asked Power.

"No," said Beresford. "But maybe training us up, just in case, might be a good idea."

"In case what?" asked Power.

"I don't know," said Beresford. "In case of a national emergency or something. You have to be prepared for emergencies don't you?"

Alleyn had returned and proffered the signing-in book to Lynch, "Sign in will you, Chief?" He watched as Lynch signed his name. "Lynch. Didn't the papers make a joke about that? When you were on the Ley Man case? The Lynch Mob – that was the headline." Alleyn didn't see Lynch frowning, or he pretended not to see. "Yes, the Lynch Mob."

"That was most superficial, unfortunate and unhelpful of the press," said Lynch, passing the book and pen to Dr Power. "Why did they reduce a potentially serious report on someone else's tragedy, which could have helped the justice process, to a simple minded pun on my name? Incidentally, Carl, did you know where the phrase 'lynch mob' comes from?"

Power had passed the signing-in book to Beresford and Alleyn collected the completed book from him after he had signed. "No, I don't. Where does it come from?"

"The Lynch name is found in England and Ireland. Probably from a Norman family, de Lench. But the phrase 'to lynch someone' probably comes from a branch of the family in Galway – James Lynch was a judge or Mayor who tried and convicted his own son for murder, and when no-one would carry out the sentence, hung his own son. Unhappy stuff. There was a Thomas Lynch in America who was equally zealous and unforgiving during the American War of Independence, but that was about three hundred years afterwards."

"So the Lynch's have always been sticklers for the law, eh?" said Alleyn, showing them through into a cold, dark room. He clicked the lights on and Power gasped. As the lights flickered on, the room seemed to lengthen and the perspective drew Power's eye down the gallery towards a small row of white targets at the furthest end. He could hardly see them. Alleyn was watching Power's expression. "One hundred metres, Dr Power. Our officers have to be able to hit a man with a carbine at one hundred metres."

"I can hardly even see the targets!" said Power.

"Stay here gentlemen, I will get you some vests and headphones." Alleyn disappeared into the armoury behind the range. He clicked some switches and adjusted the lighting so that there was just a glow of light at the far end of the range and some 80 metres of darkness between.

Power turned to Lynch, "An Irish ancestry? Power is an Irish name too."

"It's complicated though," said Lynch. "I did some work on the family tree, but couldn't get beyond the eighteenth century. And all the Lynch's in the family I traced were in England. Though of course they could have come across from Ireland. Or been here in England all the time."

"Snap," said Power. "The Powers could have been part of the Normans who invaded Wexford in Ireland. Or they could have been English and the name derived from them being poor or miserly."

Lynch laughed. "Our ancestors might have been brothers in arms."

"Or on different sides? It depends on your point of view," said Power. "I guess that we'll never know whose side our ancestors were on. I just hope we aren't letting them down . . . what would they think of us?"

Alleyn had returned with a trolley load of equipment. He proceeded to push this down through the darkness towards the light. "I hope I've got everything," he said. "It's a long way back. We're going to the twenty metre line."

They trooped after Alleyn as he wheeled the trolley through the darkness. They moved towards the target area.

"Where does the surname Beresford come from?" Power asked Beresford, Lynch's trusted Sergeant.

"English through and through I think," Beresford said. "I've never checked."

"Right gentleman," said Alleyn, drawing to a halt by a line marked '20m'. "This is where we make a stand." Hang your coats and stuff up on the pegs on the wall and come and put one of these on. He handed them each a bullet proof vest. Power was surprised by how heavy it was. "Safety first, gentlemen." Next he handed out some goggles and ear protectors. "You can put the goggles on, but don't put the ear defenders on yet. Or you won't be able to hear the instructions."

"What's in these?" asked Power, pointing to the vests. "Lead?"

"Kevlar, Doctor. It's a synthetic fibre. Right," said Alleyn. "Let's run through some stuff. I have brought out one weapon. That means we shoot in turn, which is slow, but it's also safer to keep an eye on any novices. Just one gun to dodge," he laughed. "I also brought the emergency trauma pack down with us, because some of us are complete novices and I'm taking no chances." He looked at Power and, amused by his own joke, laughed again. Power frowned.

"The armed police usually employ three weapons, Dr Power, a rubber baton round gun – it fires rubber bullets. They are meant to be non-lethal and can be used to control riots or similar. I can't say they are 100% non-lethal though. There have been a few fatalities . . . freak accidents. I hear they're experimenting with an electric gun in the US, and that may be an alternative we see in the future – it shoots out darts which deliver a high voltage shock that disables someone momentarily."

"Sounds barbaric," said Power.

"Might be safer than these baton rounds, who knows?" said Alleyn, and handed Power an example of a rubber bullet. It was a small plastic cylinder with a squashy end and weighed a few ounces.

"It's heavier than I thought," said Power.

"It's fired from over thirty-three metres away," said Alleyn. "Any closer it can do a deal of damage." He retrieved the round from Power.

"Then we also have the carbine rifle. We use the Heckler-Koch G36. Officers have to achieve body shots at one hundred metres. It can overheat if over-used, but for our limited use it's fine."

Power thought how he could only just discern the targets at that range. He looked at the six targets ahead of him at twenty metres.

The outlines of human figures on the white boards were clear. He could make out the inner rings that would circle round the figure's hearts, if they had any.

"Our officers need rapid decision making skills and to be motivated and self-confident. Because when their fingers are on the trigger they are about 8 lbs worth of pressure away from killing someone. And the handgun we will use today is a Glock. It's a polymer-framed, short recoil operated, locked breech semi-automatic pistol. Been used in police forces around the world over the last decade or so. We use the Glock 19 and it fires 9mm cartridges." Alleyn handed a spent cartridge to Power, who looked at the bottom, saw the word 'Luger' and mused about soldiers, and watching black and white Second World War films when he was a child. His attention had drifted and was drawn back to Alleyn who was looking directly at Power. "This is most important, Doctor." Alleyn re-capped the safety points he had been making. He showed Power the magazine clip, the metal slide on the top of the firearm. "The clip has numbers on it. They always face towards the back of the firearm. The notch should always face forward. It slides in and you hear a click." He demonstrated. "You release it by pressing the button here near the trigger. You must check the gun is unloaded, even if you take the clip out. There could still be a round in it. You pull the slide back and if there is a round inside it will be ejected from the port on the top. NEVER pull the trigger to check if the gun is unloaded. That sounds obvious, but people do. When you pull the slide back you should be able to look down all the way through the pistol from the top, down where the clip was and beyond. That's how you know it's unloaded." He then showed Power how to load the gun with a loaded clip and prepare the first round using the slide, and how the gun would automatically take the next round up after firing until the clip was empty. Alleyn then explained even more, how to wear the pistol, draw it ('a straight draw'), the positions for shooting, and various homilies about health and safety. Then, he asked the company to stand back, put their ear defenders on, and he loaded a clip with seven cartridges in. As they watched he fired all six shots in a strict rhythm, pumping them into a fresh target at position one. This done, Alleyn unloaded the weapon, checked the gun was truly empty and put it down. To Power, Alleyn seemed slightly breathless, over and above what might be expected. Alleyn beckoned them and they walked with him to the target. Alleyn counted out the six holes in the target. All fell closely within the inner target. Alleyn smiled.

"And now you Andrew, let's see you load the clip up and we will see how you do." Lynch did not want to be beaten and loaded the clips swiftly and precisely. He looked up at Alleyn, "Do you want me to put the clip in the pistol?"

"Yes, stand back people. Load the pistol Andrew, and move to target two. I don't want you claiming my hits. Ear defenders please."

They moved back and Lynch fired. He paused after each shot, looking at the target. At the end, Lynch checked and doubled checked the gun was empty. They went over to scrutinize his efforts. Four hits in the inner circle. Two hovered around the left shoulder. "Well done," said Alleyn. " We'll see how you do with a bit of practice. You were standing too stiffly at the start for those first two. Okay, we'll come back to you in a tick . Let's move on to target three. Who's up next? Doctor." Power shrank back hoping that Beresford would take his place, but Alleyn was proffering him the empty pistol. "Let's see you load the clip and load the Glock."

Power took the weapon gingerly. It was heavy, but not as heavy as he had imagined. He fumbled his way through loading the clip. Alleyn helped him. "It can seem a bit stiff at first. Don't be afraid of the bullets, they won't go off with the pressure of your hand." Alleyn seemed a bit wheezy.

"Are you all right?" asked Power.

"A touch of asthma," said Alleyn. "It's not usually a problem. It's usually cats that trigger it and there are none around here." Power looked around the scrupulously clean concrete interior of the range. Not a speck of dust or dirt. "Come on, Doctor, stop dawdling."

Power was aware that Lynch and Beresford had already stepped back him as he took his turn. He noticed they'd moved much further away than they had for Alleyn and wondered how dangerous they thought he really was. He crossed to the third shooting position as marked on the twenty metre line. He deliberately, and very carefully, walked holding the gun so that it pointed away from anybody. Standing at the third position he put himself into the shooting stance he had been taught. There was a cough from Alleyn. "Ear defenders, Dr Power!" Power had forgotten. He hitched the ear protectors into place awkwardly, with one hand. He looked over at Alleyn. Alleyn had his hand over his mouth, as if he was coughing or something. But he nodded at Power to begin and Power turned his attention to the shooting and to the target in front of him. He took aim and shot. The recoil thrummed through his arm. He staggered back a bit and altered his stance to be more stable. He shot the last five rounds steadily, feeling the bullets clicking upwards inside the clip automatically as the internal mechanism of the pistol reloaded for him. And then he was done. He wandered over to the target rather elatedly, surprised at the pleasure of finding all six holes in the target were clustered within the inner circle. He was suddenly aware that no one was standing with him, admiring his success, and turned round puzzled and took his ear defenders off.

Lynch and Beresford were kneeling by Alleyn's prone body, bending over him.

Superintendent Lynch was shouting, "Carl!"

Power felt his heart falling into his boots. How had he shot

Alleyn? A ricochet? He felt a hot apprehension colour his face as he struggled with a mixture of alarm, fear and concern. "I can't have shot him? I didn't mean . . ."

He ran over.

"It's not you," said Lynch. "You were firing well away from us, but he just gasped and crumpled."

"It's not a bullet?" Power asked, placing the gun down.

"No, come and look at him Carl, please. I think he's dying. He can't seem to breathe."

Power dropped to Alleyn's right hand side and took Alleyn's carotid pulse. It was fast. Power estimated 112 beats per minute. A tachycardia. Alleyn's skin was covered in a sheen of sweat. Alleyn was still conscious, but could seemingly not talk or breathe much. His skin was growing dusky and blue. The veins in his neck were distended. "Are you in pain?" Alleyn managed to point somehow to his left chest. "The pain's there?" Alleyn nodded feebly.

"What's wrong?" asked Lynch.

"Shh," said Power. "I'm thinking." Power struggled to find his way through diagnostic systems that had become somewhat rusty. He had spent a year on a cardiothoracic ward as a Registrar. But it was a while ago. He turned to Beresford. "Ring for an ambulance, NOW! Go on."

Beresford stood up began to run down the long shooting range. His feet echoed on the concrete floor.

Power looked back down to Alleyn's chest. It was hardly moving and yet seemed barrel-like, over-inflated. His thoughts began to click into place and he pulled Alleyn's collar and tie open. He pushed his index and middle finger into the collar and felt in to the midline, at the bottom of Alleyn's neck, for the suprasternal notch. He felt for the trachea and with academic satisfaction found the windpipe, which should have been central, and not deviated over towards the right, as it was.

He looked at Lynch. "We can't wait for an ambulance, he will be dead if we do. It's a tension pneumothorax."

"What's that?"

"It's a build up of pressure in the pleural space . . . squeezing his lungs like a sponge . . . down to almost nothing. He's on the edge of an arrest. I need a chest drain or . . . get me the trauma pack, Andrew." Power hoped that the shooting range emergency kit would carry something a bit more heavy duty than a few plasters and a bandage or two. His friend scrambled over to the trolley, running into it in his haste. It rolled away slightly. Power was pulling off the bulletproof vest, pulling Alleyn's shirt aside, exposing his chest. Lynch sagged down onto his knees by Power, opening the trauma pack to help. In Lynch's haste the contents spilled over Alleyn's body and the concrete floor.

"Sorry, sorry," muttered Lynch as Power scanned the fallen contents.

"Thank God," said Power as he focused on a small packet with a needle and cannula in. "A grey venflon, brilliant!" Power ripped open an alcohol swab and wiped the left side of Alleyn's chest. He deftly unwrapped the long needle, felt for the second rib space on the left hand side, and plunged the needle down through the skin and intercostal muscle. By his side, Lynch gasped.

Power pulled the needle out from the plastic housing and the plastic tube or cannula that was now inserted into Alleyn's chest. There was, to Power's mind, a most satisfying whistle of air, as the air that had built up inside Alleyn's chest cavity under pressure – now began to issue forth. Gratifyingly, as the pressure in Alleyn's thorax fell, the veins in Alleyn's neck began to improve. Inside his chest, Power hoped there would now be at least some room for his lungs to expand into. And as Alleyn struggled to draw breath, Power saw his chest moving up and down – a small way at first, then gradually gasping, shuddering mini-breaths.

Alleyn struggled to speak. "Oh, oh, that's better Dr Power. What's wrong?"

"Stay still, don't speak. Has this ever happened before?" Alleyn shook his head. "Do you smoke?" Alleyn nodded. "Well you won't be smoking from now on," said Power. "It is a risk factor. You've had what's called a tension pneumothorax. It's rare. We need to get you to hospital now."

Alleyn struggled to say, "I can hardly breathe still."

"I know; you need a proper chest drain and valve set up. The venflon was the best I could find, I'm afraid. But it is enough to save your life."

Beresford was sprinting back down the range towards them. He looked down at Alleyn and the small contraption sticking out of his chest. "He's alive then?"

Lynch nodded, "Thanks to Dr Power."

"Not bad for a psychologist," said Beresford.

"I'm not a psychologist," said Power. "I'm medically trained."

"A proper doctor then?" asked Beresford.

"Of course he's a proper doctor, Sergeant," said Lynch. "Where's the ambulance?"

"The ambulance is on its way," said Beresford. "It's being escorted through by uniform."

"Well done, Carl," said Lynch patting his friend's shoulder.

Power was half-listening and carefully putting a couple of jackets over Alleyn's bare chest, avoiding the life saving cannula as he did. He wanted to keep Alleyn warm. "And I got six shots on target," Power grinned.

The Artist
February 1995

There was a parking space temporarily reserved for Power behind the gallery in Deansgate, Manchester. He eased his battered Saab into place and cut the engine. Given the difficulties Power had endured in starting the engine before his journey he wondered if the engine would start when he wanted to go home. The day was bitterly cold and a thin film of ice clung to every outdoor surface. The sky was leaden and the piercing wind blew straight through Power's jacket which seemed to offer as little warmth as if he was standing naked on the cobbled street.

He scurried round to the front of the gallery and tried to push open the door. It was locked and a hastily scribbled biro note taped to the surface of the inner glass said, 'Closed today due to unforeseen emergency.'

Power rang the doorbell and tried to remember the last time he had been to the Gallery. It must have been the opening of a show three or four years ago. He had been Eve's guest. He remembered it had been near Halloween. There had been pumpkin lanterns all over the gallery and soup made from their flesh, which he detested as being tasteless and bland. But it had been warm and bright inside then and now here he was, shivering on the threshold, wondering why he had responded to Eve's summons. They had hardly spoken more than a few words since her abandonment of him one Christmas. Why had he responded to her call for help now?

Peering through the gallery front window, Power could not discern any activity now in the dark grey interior of the gallery. Then

all of a sudden he saw Eve emerging from a door at the rear of the gallery. She made her way over to let him in. She looked thinner than he remembered her. Pale. Dressed in some handknitted dress that did not flatter the figure he had once made love to. Her eyes were watery and she gave him the briefest of smiles of reassurance as she unlocked the door bolts at top and bottom.

He hurried past her, eager to get into the warmth. They looked at each other, both clearly embarrassed. She essayed a hug, but all they could manage was an unco-ordinated flurry of arms and elbows. Awkward. They stood on the polished concrete floor and mumbled formal greetings.

"Thank you for coming, Carl. I know that you didn't need to . . ."

"It's fine," he said. He looked around at the walls. "Between exhibitions?" he asked.

"No," she said. "There were paintings there. They're the ones that were taken." She pointed to a large and empty easel that stood on Power's right. "That was the main attraction. A painting by Lowry."

"I'm not Lowry's biggest fan," confessed Power. "Am I the right person to help? I mean, not because I don't like Lowry . . . I mean, where are the police? If paintings have been stolen?"

"It's complicated," said Eve. "It was an exhibition of twentieth century Salford artists."

"I don't know any apart from Lowry and his depressing stick men," said Power. He thought over what he had just said and wondered if he sounded a bit bitter. Was his anger towards her showing through?

"Oh, he's not the only one. There are some sculptures by Randall and paintings by Harold Riley too – we've got a portrait by Riley of Lowry himself." She pointed over to a canvas in the corner.

"It's better than anything by Lowry," said Power dismissively, glancing at it.

Eve frowned. She knew Power could be difficult if he wanted to be. She badly didn't want an argument. She was so close to tears in any event.

"Would you like a cup of tea?" she asked.

"Milky coffee if you have it. No sugar."

"I remember," she said. She led him to the door at the rear of the gallery. "The kitchen's through here."

"I remember too," said Power. "Are you still painting?"

"A bit," said Eve. "I'm mainly managing this place these days. At least it pays."

She took him into the small galley of a kitchen, made two cups of coffee, and led him through to her office. To Power's surprise there was a man slumped over the desk. He did not acknowledge their entry, and rested his head on his forearms on the desk, quiet and still. Eve saw Power's surprise as she placed one mug of coffee down by an empty seat for Power and placed the other mug near the silent man. "Mind the coffee I made you, Simon. It's by your elbow. Don't knock it." She looked at Power. "Simon's in shock, I think. He owns the gallery. Do you remember him?" Power was not sure. They must have met, he supposed.

"Hello," said Power to the silent man. There was no response, but Power could see he was still breathing. His back was moving gently up and down. He looked questioningly at Eve. Simon lifted his head for an instant and regarded Power impassively. He was older than Power. His hair was silver-grey and his features were thicker set, almost rubbery. His eyes were blue and steely. One eye was bruised and there was a cut on his forehead, which was still fresh. "You could maybe do with a stitch in that, or a steri-strip at least," said Power.

"It will do," said Simon and disappeared into his own world once more, sinking his head on to his arms.

"He doesn't want anything formal," said Eve. "No accident and emergency. No police. No publicity. It would be too damaging."

"But if a Lowry has been stolen . . ."

"Several Lowry paintings," corrected Eve.

"Then surely that is a theft – costing millions?"

Eve sighed and glanced over at Simon for help. Only the top of his curly haired head was visible, and he was silent. "We don't want publicity because it was the artist himself who came here, took the paintings and assaulted Simon."

"What?" Power objected. "Lowry's been dead for about twenty years."

"You're right, Carl, he's been dead almost *exactly* twenty years," said Eve.

Power felt confused. His confusion was not assisted by his sudden notice of a simple bunch of red roses in a vase and without meaning to he had read that they were to Eve from Simon. Adding this to the knowledge that it had only recently been Valentine's Day, and Power found he was thinking about Eve's new relationship rather than the puzzle of the return of Lowry's ghost.

Eve thought Power's evident confusion was to do with the paintings and their artist rather than the revelation that Eve and Simon were lovers. "We were so sure that the paintings were genuine, Carl. But they were forgeries."

Power's brain clicked into a solution of the puzzle. "So, the artist that returned to get the paintings was the forger?"

"Yes," Eve smiled at Power's misunderstanding. It was the first genuine smile she had given him that day. "We were selling the paintings for him. Not as the artist, obviously. We thought he was the owner, not the artist, as it turned out. He assured us of their provenance. He was so convincing. We even took expert advice. So, as he owned them and took them back before they were sold, I suppose he can't be accused of stealing paintings that he owned. And as we hadn't sold them yet, there was no fraud either."

Simon's head rose from the table and his voice was loud and strong. "And if we told anybody, if there was publicity . . . how would we look? Like idiots at best, or at worst – criminals ourselves. And no one would trust us ever, ever again. The art world is all about image, about trust. And we would never be trusted again. Finished. Forever finished."

"And that's why we really wanted to talk to you, Carl . . ."

"Did he attack you, Simon?" asked Power. "You could bring charges?"

"There was a confrontation, yes. I think I gave as good as I got," said Simon. "And I do need to emphasise that we DO NOT need any publicity. We couldn't afford to involve the police formally."

"So what led to the 'confrontation'?" asked Power.

"It's unbelievable," Simon shook his head. "A nightmare. We had one expert from the bloody University. Another expert who swore he knew every painting that Lowry ever painted. They both signed certificates as to the validity of these four paintings. Then last night – the night before we opened the doors on the exhibition – Eve takes a magnifying glass to the paintings. Three of them are paintings of mills and stickmen. The last was a self-portrait of Lowry as an old man. Side on. Hat, Macintosh, jowls. There's a bloody newspaper sticking out of his pocket. You can read it. The *Manchester Evening News*. Look close and it's dated 24th February 1977." Power looked puzzled. Simon scowled, "Lowry died in 1976. The artist was marking the paintings as fakes."

"It was a shock," said Eve. "I looked at the others. There were these small, really tiny mistakes. Deliberate errors. Like in the crowd of mill workers leaving at the end of the day, in a painting supposedly from 1930, there's one tiny figure near the gates. If you look carefully enough he's holding a mobile phone to his ear." She looked to be on the edge of tears. "Simon had given the owner an advance of £200,000 on the basis of the certificates of authenticity."

"He gave the cheque back this morning," said Simon. "He hadn't cashed it, hadn't spent a penny. He came to retrieve the paintings so I couldn't take them anywhere I suppose. He didn't want to go to prison. The money wasn't the point for him. I was so angry with him – livid – that we had a fight. It was over very quickly. Clearly neither of us have had much experience as fighters."

"It was rather comical to watch," said Eve. "A sort of flapping at each other."

"I punched him," said Simon. "Hard. But he got the four paintings into his estate car nevertheless and he drove off at high speed. Nearly hit two cars."

"How do you think I can help?" said Power. Presumably it's not my surgical skills you were interested in?"

"The owner of the paintings is mad," said Simon.

"We think he's the painter, too," said Eve. "We thought you might help."

"It's not like I collect these people," said Dr Power. "By and large these people come to me for help. Of their own volition usually. I don't think that this man . . ."

". . . he calls himself Lord Emlyn of Woolton."

Power tried not to smile.

"He was very convincing," said Eve, pouting.

"Confidence tricksters always are," said Power. "But there's something more at play here. As you implied earlier, it wasn't about the money. He was quite happy to bring that back, especially to preserve his freedom. It isn't money that motivates him."

"Then what?" asked Eve.

"He got what he wanted," said Power. "Lord Emlyn's motivation, like many forgers, was to prove to himself that he was better than your experts, and therefore, in his eyes at least, as good as a major artist like Lowry. If he could pass off one of his paintings as a Lowry to an expert, he had won. I presume they were quite good fakes?"

"Indistinguishable from the real thing," said Simon, his head back on his arms. "I will have to ask the PR and events people to put out a press release to cover the cancellation tonight."

"Carl, we want to ask you to help. You seem to know at least a bit about what makes Lord Emlyn tick. We want you to retrieve something for us. It would save our reputation. We will pay, or make a donation to a charity of your choice if you agree."

Power wondered what she meant. "He has the paintings. You have your money. There's no loss, probably no crime can be proven. What's left?"

"The paintings had our validation – a certificate of authenticity signed by us and our two experts – pasted to the back. He could take the paintings to anyone. Sell them almost anywhere on the strength of our say-so, and then when the questions arose, when the shit hit the fan, the phone here would ring and they'd ask why did you validated these paintings. They might want damages. Our reputation would be dragged through the dirt. Do you see what we have at stake?"

"Maybe you could argue that the certificates – like the paintings – were fakes?" asked Power.

"But we know they are not fake certificates, Carl. *We know.* And whether they are real or fake our name would be dragged into Lord Emlyn's mad little world. We must have them back."

"And you think that I can get them back because I know his mind?"

"I know you, Carl."

"And a donation to charity if I do?" asked Power. Eve nodded. "Okay," agreed Power, smiling. "I accept the challenge."

* * *

The self-styled Lord Emlyn took the last bubble-wrapped painting out of the estate car and closed the rear door. He carried the painting gently across the Square and into the Old Hall Hotel, Buxton.

There had been a downstairs room, a private dining room, booked for him to use and he propped the last painting onto one of the four easels that had been arranged on a vast Georgian dining table to display the paintings to his client.

The Old Hall Hotel had seen many customers since the 16th Century, but few as pompous and exquisitely dressed as Lord Emlyn. He was dressed in a suit of the finest Harris Tweed, with a soft linen shirt and turquoise silk cravat. He was subtly perfumed in a scent created for him by Jo Malone and sent up from a small boutique in London. He looked at the placement of the four Lowry paintings and moved one subtly to his satisfaction. Emlyn then took out a folder and extracted the four certificates of authenticity and placed them on the table, each in front of the respective painting.

Emlyn wondered about the expert who had made the appointment with him. He'd phoned and introduced himself as Dr Steingrimur, and said he was with the Tate Icelandic Consortium. Dr Steingrimur had said he represented a group of Icelandic finance houses who wanted to invest in art. His Icelandic accent was distinctive, but quite faint. He was in the Northwest – seeing a painting in Derbyshire, on a visit to the Cavendish family at Chatsworth House. He had several million to invest, and was also looking out for donations to the Reykjavik Art Museum. Dr Steingrimur had heard via a contact in London that Emlyn had inherited some Lowry paintings and wanted to see them. Dr Steingrimur could offer him accommodation in Buxton, which wasn't too far from Chatsworth. It would be more convenient for Steingrimur than a visit to Manchester.

Lord Emlyn had been particularly intrigued by the mention of the Reykjavik Art Museum, and accepted Dr Steingrimur's kind invitation to afternoon tea at the Old Hall Hotel in Buxton.

True to his word Dr Steingrimur had arranged a pleasant room with good light to display the paintings. The good doctor had also organised coffee and tea. Some sandwiches nestled nearby, under a glass dome to keep them fresh. There looked to be salmon and cucumber, and tomato and avocado. Under a second dome were four cream scones, oozing raspberry jam. A plate of bread and butter and a jar of honey accompanied the tea. Lord Emlyn smiled and hoped that Dr Steingrimur would be on time so they could eat as soon as possible. His mouth was watering.

On the dot of 2.30 p.m., as promised, there was a crisp knock on the door and Dr Steingrimur breezed into the room, smiling.

Lord Emlyn looked Steingrimur up and down – a fact which did not escape Steingrimur's keen and twinkling eyes. Emlyn saw a smartly dressed man in a dark blue suit, slim and lithe. He was younger than Lord Emlyn had imagined. Despite his relative youth and absence of grey from his unruly dark hair, Dr Steingrimur seemed self-assured, though not arrogant. Steingrimur's eyes were locked onto Emlyn's face and somehow seemed to delve deep into Emlyn's soul. But Steingrimur was offering reassurance, a hand stretched out in friendship and a broad, confident grin. Emlyn noticed Steingrimur's warm and distinctive cologne as he entered the private room.

"Lord Emlyn, thank you so much for meeting me on this part of my tour. I've heard about your collection and your generosity to various museums over the years. It is such a pleasure to meet you." The gaze drifted to the paintings and back to Emlyn's face. "I see that you have brought a few paintings to meet me! Have you had anything to eat or drink? No? Please start while I look at the paintings. Perhaps you can talk to me as you refresh yourself?" Steingrimur suddenly had a magnifying glass in his hand and was no longer at Emlyn's side, but was peering intently at the paintings. Lord Emlyn poured himself a cup of coffee and removed some salmon sandwiches from under the glass. He munched contentedly as Steingrimur made a range of appreciative noises. "You have the certificates of authenticity. Hardly necessary. I believe you knew Lowry?"

"My family knew him. I was small at the time, but he would pat me on the head. He was always in a fawn Mac. My Dad always drove Mr Lowry on his holidays. My Mum would bake him cakes, scones like these as a matter of fact. Emlyn pointed at the cream scones nearby. Steingrimur watched Emlyn as he munched and boasted. He gave us pictures over the years."

"I have heard that Lowry did this, yes," said Steingrimur. "He wasn't precious about his paintings."

"These are just four of around twelve paintings that my family got. I developed the art collecting bug over the years. I became a banker myself, like your clients, and bought a few artworks by other painters and sold them at a profit, and so it went, getting more valuable works, by more famous artists each time. It's a hobby with me, like. And it funds itself, because it's profitable."

"You have a good eye," said Steingrimur. "But you hung onto the Lowry's till now, eh?"

"Sentimental value," said Emlyn. "They remind me of happier times with my Mum and Dad. We weren't grand. My Dad would never have believed his son would be made a Lord for services to the Finance Industry."

"I suppose he wouldn't," said Steingrimur, without irony. He picked up the first certificate and compared it to the painting. "This has been recently certified," Steingrimur noted. "Were you hoping to sell perhaps?"

"I thought maybe to loan one or two long-term, better that many people see them, that they be displayed and enjoyed in a gallery rather than buried in my apartment."

Steingrimur nodded. "Think of giving not only as a duty but as a privilege. Isn't that what they say."

"Of course," said Emlyn, but wasn't sure what the slim Icelander really meant.

Steingrimur appraised the first painting, *"The Millworkers Depart,* painted in 1930, on board, 600mm x 300mm, owned by your good self, insurance value £800,000. Good, good, a typical Lowry subject. Before the robots took their jobs eh?" He moved to the second painting and matched the certificate to it. "*Punch and Judy at Heaton Park, Manchester,* painted in 1918 on canvas, 300mm x 300mm, owned by you, insurance value £660,000 – look at those soldiers in the crowd of spectators, the ones who survived the First World War probably. I bet they'd seen a deal more than Mr Punch's violence. Such a waste of life." Steingrimur moved to the next painting and rubbed his chin. "A self-portrait from 1972. Mr Lowry reading the newspaper – he looks like he needs a shave, himself! Insurance value is £900,000. On canvas. 300mm x 300mm, again. A popular size." He moved to the final painting "The last one now. A picture of shops, a view from Station Road on wood, painted 1969, 287mm x 140mm, valued at £250,000."

"That's just over the road from where Lowry lived. I ran down there as a boy to buy him a paper."

Steingrimur grinned and even went so far as to clasp Lord Emlyn's hand in both of his and shake it warmly. "Fantastic. Lovely to have this detail from Mr Lowry's own friend! Amazing. Well these are brilliant examples of Lowry's work. They show such skill."

Steingrimur's steely eyes noticed Emlyn smiling at this. "Of course, I'm not a great fan of Lowry, but I can see that these are *better* than much of his work. And we'd love to house these at the Museum, absolutely. We have a new building planned near the Harbour – it will be called the Hafnarhús. That's where we hope to house a new collection of paintings like these. I am collecting for the new building now. That's if you ever felt like making a loan or a donation, of course. And we'd be so grateful for your donation. You would become an Honorary Fellow of our Museum, yes, and you would be welcome to visit the museum every year at our expense." But at this point Dr Steingrimur paused and seemed to frown ever so slightly, almost imperceptibly. He had become seemingly fascinated by a point on the self-portrait's canvas. "Although, Lord Emlyn, some of our experts would undoubtedly notice that the date on the newspaper Lowry is reading is for the year after Lowry died and that over here on the millworkers' scene they might notice that the mill worker is carrying a mobile phone, and that here on this other painting from 1918, there is a car on the roadside near the edge of the crowd – a creamy beige Austin 7 with a black roof. You see what I mean here? Austin didn't start production of the Austin 7 until 1922. You've incorporated some deliberate mistakes in your work, haven't you?"

Steingrimur swivelled to face Lord Emlyn. "I'm sorry, but I'm no more Dr Steingrimur than this painting is by Lowry, or you are really a Lord." Lord Emlyn's mouth was agape. He noticed how Steingrimur had changed physically as he confronted Emlyn. The accent, stance and even the movements of the man had changed. Emlyn wouldn't have been surprised if he, Steingrimur, had actually shed his skin. Emlyn was momentarily stunned as the man who was Dr Power went on. "You hate the art world don't you? You think you are more talented, and a deal more clever than us all."

Growling, Emlyn started gathering the paintings and the certificates together in a hurried frenzy. His brow was furrowed in rage.

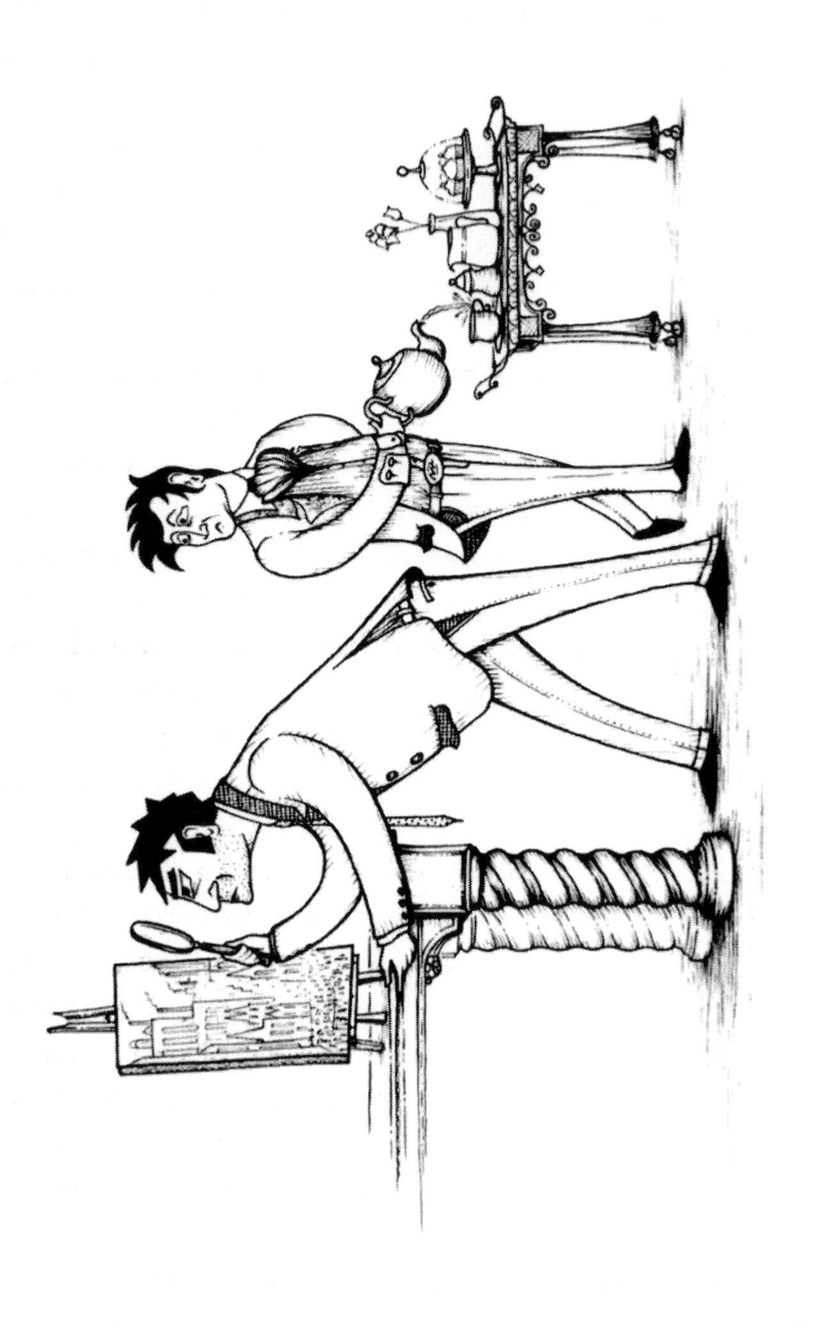

"I think you'd better leave them here, don't you?" asked Dr Power.

"They're mine, Dr Steingrimur, or whoever you really are. I haven't sold them. I haven't committed any crime. I can do what I like."

"My name is Dr Power. I am a psychiatrist. If you won't leave the paintings, then I certainly want the certificates back, please. **They** really don't belong to you, and if I let you keep them you will damage my friends and their business every time you show these forgeries to people."

"They were fool enough to write and sign them. They belong to me. And the paintings are originals, not forgeries."

"No," said Dr Power. "I can't let you take the certificates."

Clutching all four paintings and the certificates under one arm Emlyn threw a heavy punch with the other arm, which Power dodged with considerable speed and grace. But Lord Emlyn dived forward with brute force and deliberately collided with Power pushing him backwards. Off balance, Power fell backwards into a wingback chair and was momentarily winded, which was all that Emlyn needed.

Emlyn dashed over to the door and was about to exit when the door opened of its own accord. The tall and imposing figure of Superintendent Lynch stood in the doorway and loomed over Emlyn. Lynch fished in his jacket pocket and flashed his warrant card. "This warrant card is just about the only real thing in this room. My name is Superintendent Lynch. Now, shall we go back inside and sit down, Mr Newton. That is your real name. You're not Lord Emlyn. And Mr Newton, I'd hate to have to arrest you for the assault on my friend, Dr Power." The former Lord Emlyn stepped backward towards the table of empty easels. Lynch entered the room and quietly closed the door behind him.

Lynch looked at Newton from under slightly hooded eyes. He looked like a man who would brook absolutely no nonsense. His broad shoulders looked powerful and Newton judged him to be in prime condition. Lynch took charge. "You're not under arrest, Mr Newton. You're not under caution, yet. So, if you think about it, I think you'll find that my colleague's suggestion of handing the certificates over is eminently sensible. Hand them over and you are free to go. Refuse, and I can guarantee there **will** be a problem, and your little fantasy will end with you behind bars."

"This is nothing but entrapment! You can't stop me leaving," blustered Newton, but in his heart of hearts he knew he was beaten.

Lynch nodded to his friend, "Are you all right, Carl? I heard the scuffle."

"I'm fine, Andrew, but thank you for coming in when you did." Power turned to the erstwhile Lord Emlyn. "Why don't you sit down and finish your tea. We can have a talk before you hand the certificates over. You know I wasn't lying when I said you do have a real talent as an artist," said Power. "So, why don't you exhibit your own work under your own name?"

"As little Mr Newton. Little Mr Nobody? Mr 'no friends in high up places'? Mr 'no agent, no contacts, no publicity'?" He poured himself a fresh cup of coffee from the tray on the table and sagged into a chair. He was trying to regain his urbane composure. If he gained control of himself, he might yet gain control of the situation. Lynch hovered at the doorway, however, effectively barring any possibility of Newton's escape. "I did plenty of my own work, but Mr Newton was never acceptable to the art world. It's a world of snobs, built on luck and who you know. A talent for self publicity is valued more than technical skill or artistic merit. And in these days celebrity counts for more than talent. If Lowry was starting out now and he turned up to that snobby effete gallery in swanky Deansgate – shuffled in wearing his greasy, grubby mac with his paintings under his arm in a brown paper parcel tied with string they'd call security and have him removed like some unwanted piece of shit. They can't see talent until it's announced as a good thing by some overpaid critic with a megaphone. I decided to let that world see that I could do anything by the Masters; that I was as good as any of them, and that they could be fooled. In fact, to prove to them that they were fools."

Power couldn't resist making an interpretation. "So it's all about your hurt? About the rejection of your original work, and how you rationalize that their rejection doesn't matter, because the judgment . . . the decision to reject you is made by fools? If you can prove they are fools, then somehow they were wrong to reject you?"

Newton sighed. "Spare me all the pop psychology, Doctor. I play Lowry, you play Freud. Is that the game? Tell me, what's so bad about what I've done? What's so bad about exposing their hypocrisy? Because you can't defend them. They aren't victims. They don't know what a good piece of art is? Most of them could **never** tell a real Lowry from a fake Lowry. Even when I put in a deliberate mistake, most people cannot see it. They are that incompetent, or greedy. And you know I usually just donate the works to galleries. They accept them and hang them up. I love that you know. I've got Lowry paintings across America; Pollocks, Dalis Rothkos and Manets, even a Titian. I am challenging the art world about what art is. That challenge I make to their cosy, anal world of money, that challenge is my painting and the challenge is itself art. The concept of passing off a work by me as a masterpiece – that's concept art in itself. And I've never tried to sell the art. The closest I got was with that exhibition in Deansgate, but I'd never actually have taken anyone's money. I'd be too frightened to defraud anyone. I got frightened when the gallery man confronted me about fraud. I was making a point – to show them how stupid it all is. My fake art is ten times more real than their fake art world. What is wrong with what I have done? They rejected me. At least I didn't cause a World War after being rejected."

* * *

Power stood with Lynch beside him at the casement window. They were both watching Newton stow his artwork back in the estate car outside the hotel. Power looked over at the remains of the tea. Newton had confessed almost everything over coffee, sandwiches and scones. As Newton drove away he looked somewhat lighter, relaxed and relieved. Confession must have been good for his soul, thought Power, but it seemed that the process of unburdening himself to the doctor and the law man had also given Newton a marvellous appetite, because there was barely anything left for Power and Lynch to eat. Power had heard that the food was good at the Old Hall and his stomach was reminding him that it was just about teatime. He wondered if Lynch would stay for a pint of beer and some dinner in Buxton. Power thought the chances were probably very good. Power had the four certificates his mission had required him to get clutched in his hand. "I must ring Eve," he said. "She will be very pleased." With his other hand he retrieved an envelope from his inner jacket pocket and handed it to Lynch. "And this is a cheque for you, Andrew. I think there must be a Church Roof collection it can go to?"

"What's this?" Lynch raised an eyebrow. The cheque had Eve's beautifully flowing blue ink pen signature and was made out for £5,000.

"Probably our first and last reward as consulting detectives," said Power. "I said we would use it as a donation to charity. It's from a very grateful lady."

The Farm
May 1996

Dr Power had sat through most of the play, *The Misfits*, and had enjoyed it for the most part. But sitting high up in the gallery of the Royal Exchange Theatre, far above the octagonal stage, he found his head nodding with sleep. The June evening was warm, and he had been on-call the night before and spent some of the early hours of the morning sitting in the Accident and Emergency Department with a blonde young woman who had been rescued from the river. She had been trying to drown herself. He had been fascinated by the slow drips that fell from her blanket-cocooned figure onto the lino floor. She had refused to speak to him and he had sat for some time trying his best to establish a rapport, until at last she had disclosed that she had also taken a paracetamol overdose, at which point Power had advised she be returned to the physician on call for treatment. He promised he would see her again when she had completed her N-acetyl-cysteine therapy and drove back home to slump into his bed.

* * *

In the theatre, warm and quiet in the gallery seats, Power was fighting against his tiredness from the night before. Down below him the actors played out the filming of Marilyn Monroe's last film, *The Misfits*. As a strange quirk of fate, the playwright Arthur Miller was being depicted by an actor in the play. Power had treated himself to a good meal in a Japanese noodle bar before the play, where he also drank a warm bowl of sake. This only compounded his sleepiness.

Unusually, he was without female company. Reasoning, therefore, that he only had himself to please, and that he shouldn't feel guilty about leaving.

Power disengaged himself from the audience as quietly as he could and made his way over to the white door of the exit along the green-carpeted walkway, and climbed down the red-coloured stairway to the parquet floor of the old cotton exchange.

The Royal Exchange Theatre stood like a monstrous space lander – a sort of expanded Lunar Module – in the belly of the vast classical-pillared Exchange. Above Power's head were numbered boards announcing cotton prices. The prices stood fixed and silent from the last day of trading, decades earlier. Power crept over the wooden floor, feeling as if his footsteps echoed in the vast space. The theatre was 'in the round' and the actors' dressing rooms were in screened off areas outside the skeletal theatre. Some actors sat there waiting for their cue and watched Power walking away. He felt as if he was an actor too, leaving the stage.

Power exited and skipped his way lightly down the stone steps to Cross Street. The air was still, and dusk was giving way to night. He readied to cross the road and looked away left, along the road, to Corporation Street. A red and white cargo truck crawled along the road, stopping Power's progress as he waited for it. The truck edged its way. A driver and passenger were looking around, and then, catching sight of Power, accelerated. As they passed, both occupants of the cab turned so that he could not see their faces. Power felt uneasy about them, and, as they disappeared away into the gloom tried to see the number plates, but his eyes were not keen enough and the night was falling fast. He was disquieted and stared ahead into the gathering shadows, watching the red rear lights disappearing, speeding away from the doctor's scrutiny.

Power walked quickly now, anxious to get to his car in the car park under the G-Mex Centre. As he passed the brightly lit windows of a pub near Albert Square and Waterstone's Town Hall a crowd of singing, shouting students spilled out onto the pavement, laughing and in high spirits. A pretty girl detached herself from the throng and staggered over to him. "Are you going home? Where do you live?" Power put his head down, looked away and walked on. "I was only asking for a lift!" she shouted after him. He felt guilty about his unfriendliness. He might have misread things.

Ahead a more refined crowd was spreading out of the Bridgewater Hall after a concert. The smartly dressed folk were approaching Power as he passed the old Manchester Central Station that had been transformed into an exhibition centre. Power was anxious now to reach the car park pay station before the crowd that now milled around him, heading towards their cars, beating Power to the ticket pay stations. And yet, in the distance, he suddenly spied a familiar figure and so he stopped.

He was sure it was her, Lucinda. She was tall and slimmer than when she had been his girlfriend, with long brown hair cascading around her shoulders. For a moment she turned, and her brown eyes locked with his, and then her gaze slid off him and she was actually pushing her way away from him through the crowd. Her name rose to his lips, but she was moving quickly away into the night and he had lost her. He caught one more glimpse of her. She was getting into a black taxi cab. The crowd moved in front of him and he lost sight of her. His last sight was her hand and arm as she pulled the taxi door to. And she was gone, leaving Power with an aching heart. This feeling of sudden loss surprised Power. He wouldn't have imagined that he still had feelings for her, but the proximity and sight of Lucinda had stirred something inside him.

It took Power two days to summon the courage to phone her mobile number. Two days of gathering his nerve; time to gather his thoughts and courage, and a third of a bottle of Crianza.

He sat in the hall of Alderley House by the telephone. The evening sun filtered through the stained glass of the windows and bathed him in a colourwash of light. He lifted the receiver and picked out her number.

"Hello," she replied almost immediately.

Power hesitated, and was anxiously tempted to put the phone down.

"Hello, Lucinda. It's Carl Power."

There was a very long pause.

"Carl. To what do I owe the pleasure?"

It didn't sound as if there was any pleasure at all in her voice. Carl's stomach turned over. He had realised that he still cared for Lucinda, his ex-girlfriend, when he had seen her in Manchester and now it seemed as if the phone call was a bad idea. Worse still, he began to think that his suspicion that she had actively run away from him in Manchester was right.

"I thought I caught sight of you in Manchester the other night. I was at a play. You were leaving a concert at the Bridgewater Hall."

"It wasn't a concert, Carl. The hall hasn't opened yet. It was a fundraiser event."

"For the rich and famous?"

Lucinda snorted. "I don't have any money to give them," she said. "Not after double death duties." Her recently widowed mother had been killed when Carl first knew Lucinda. At the other end of the phone from her, Power felt his self-confidence diminishing.

"Well, I thought I caught sight of you, and I wondered whether you would like dinner maybe? So we can catch up?" His words tumbled into silent space and floated into nothingness.

"It's an idea," she said, without warmth. "Normally I'd love to catch up with an old friend, but I don't know . . . so many bad things happened around you – I know it wasn't your fault – and I'm only just beginning to pull my way out of it even now."

"That's a no, then?"

"It's a not yet, Carl."

"Okay, well I'll let you go. If I can ever help you or you want to talk please let me know. Keep in touch?" He put the phone down and suddenly felt a very small man alone in the vast Victorian house that he inhabited.

* * *

Power was walking from the Countess of Chester Hospital towards the City Centre. He had a lunchtime meeting planned with his friend, Superintendent Lynch, at the Police HQ in Nuns Road. Power had left his old Saab 96 estate at the hospital and was en route, across the road from the petrol station, when again he saw someone with a familiar face, at the garage. The customer had just filled his Land Rover Defender with diesel and paid. Power waved to him as he stood on the forecourt, and clearly saw that Michael, Lucinda's brother recognised him. As if on autopilot, Michael's arm began to wave back to Power and then he corrected his arm's travel and he scowled.

By this time, however, Power was halfway across the road towards the garage in his mission to say hello to Lucinda's brother. As Power walked over the last few yards of tarmac Michael was seemingly stung into action. He hurriedly climbed up into the Land Rover and started it up. By the time Power had reached the garage forecourt, Michael's Land Rover had roared away in a cloud of grey smoke.

Power stood on the pavement watching the dusty green Land Rover disappearing up the road into town. He realised his mouth was open – and closed it. He conjectured that Michael was headed through the town and on to the village of Heaton where his parents had once lived in the sprawling estate around Heaton Hall. He began the climb up the hill into town, past the College and onto the bypass that led to the monolithic headquarters where Lynch was stationed. His mind kept replaying the moment Michael realised who he was, and Michael's scowl that had accompanied that moment of recognition.

Lynch and Power had walked from the Police headquarters along the City walls to the Albion pub for lunch. Power had the afternoon off and sipped a pint of bitter and munched on a flaky beef and ale pie, while Lynch, looking forward to an afternoon in a meeting chaired by the ever-sober Chief Constable, drank a bottle of ginger beer. Lynch stared at his friend across a plate-sized battered haddock and a mountain of chips, all dripping in vinegar. Lynch was unusually perceptive for a police officer and had picked up on his friend's vague disquiet. Interrupting his own chatter about the case they were both working on together, Lynch paused, and asked, "Are you all right, Carl?"

"Two things," said Power. "Two things are bothering me. Well, one thing really, and two people. I bumped into the two people by chance. And the one thing that bothered me is that neither would wait. They both saw me and hurried off. They couldn't face me."

"Who were they?" asked Lynch.

"Lucinda McWilliam is one and her brother Michael is the other. She saw me in Manchester and hurried off in a taxi, and her brother saw me at a petrol station just now and hurtled away in a Land Rover like he'd seen the devil or something."

Lynch frowned at the names.

Power expected his friend to be reassuring and to soothe his feelings, maybe say that the McWilliam children were both grieving and that seeing Power was some sort of symbol of their past and the events at Heaton Hall.

Instead, Lynch was uncharacteristically blunt. "I told you then, I said, 'don't have anything to do with her, or him'. You didn't listen then, and you got your fingers burned. Why don't you learn? Why don't you listen? I'm asking you now, as a friend, to steer clear of that pair. Steer clear!"

Power was taken aback at Lynch's sharp tone. He couldn't quite remember Lynch ever speaking to him in that way before. He did remember the previous warning though which, admittedly, Power had not heeded then. Lynch had warned him not to get involved with Lucinda, and what had he done? Power had taken her into his bed. Now, in the Albion pub, he blushed. "I don't understand why you are so angry," he said.

Lynch put his knife and fork down and sighed. "Not angry, Carl. Frustrated. Frightened for you." He made eye contact. "Please listen to me. Let this one go. Avoid both of them. Like . . . the . . . Plague. I can't be any clearer than that, can I?"

Power hated being told by anyone what he could and couldn't do and he remained puzzled as to his friend's motives. He wanted to probe further, but his instinct told him that Lynch had said his final word on the matter, for today at least. Power swallowed his curiosity and hurt and turned the subject of the conversation onto easier ground. Soon the friends were discussing their latest case again, and before the end of the meal there was even the return of good humour and laughter. But on his walk back down the hill alone to his car, Power's postprandial mood darkened as he tried to understand the actions of Lucinda and Michael McWilliam and his friend Andrew Lynch.

* * *

Power drove the ancient Saab out of Chester. He scarcely noticed

PRIVATE PROPERTY
DANGER
KEEP OUT

the villages and countryside as he passed by and, as if on autopilot, he found that he was on the outskirts of Heaton. He half-told himself that he hadn't meant to journey here. Nevertheless, here he was. He parked his car in a small, gravelled lay-by at the side of the road. Ahead, there was a small bridge over a river. The sense of *déjà vu* was inevitable. He had parked here once before.

There was a sandstone wall that ran all the way around the estate. Power looked about him to see if anyone was driving past or walking nearby to witness what he was about to do. He scaled the sandstone wall and dropped down to the ground on the other side. He walked softly through the trees. The shrubs and trees in the grounds had lacked any attention for years and had grown thickly. He emerged into a space that formed a clearing. Even here the grass had grown until it was past Power's knees. To his left was a driveway, littered with weeds. In the mid-distance was the old Lodge. It had been abandoned after the fire had gutted the old Hall, but the Lodge seemed inhabited. Curtains hung at the windows and the woodwork looked bright and freshly painted.

To his right the drive curved round, widened, and swept into a broad circle in front of the skeleton of the old house. The blackened bones of the old Hall loomed up into the blue May sky. Power looked up at the brick walls, roofless and stark. He shuddered, because the Hall and Power's own home, Alderley House, had been designed by the same architect. The two buildings were alike, but unlike. Power's house was a smaller version of the behemoth of a building that was Heaton Hall. Power's house was alive, but this Hall was dead. The ruin seemed as quiet as a country graveyard.

On the south side of the house Power remembered that there had been a ruin of a conservatory. The metal frame of the conservatory had been twisted and the conservatory glass had been shattered by the intense heat of the blaze.

His memory of the Hall's wreckage seemed imperfect however, because the conservatory seemed restored – a large, white structure with acres of glass had been re-built onto a wing of the Hall. Although most of the Hall was still roofless; this one wing had been largely re-built and re-roofed. Power was pleased to see the restoration, but somehow his joy was tempered by a sense of misgiving. His feeling that he had intruded into somewhere very private, and that his presence would be unwelcome, tainted his pleasure at seeing the Hall the process of being re-born.

He looked left again at the Lodge to see if anyone was watching him. He noticed that the gates beyond the Lodge were new, solid, high and firmly shut. The Hall was surrounded by a thick forest, and its borders were sealed.

He sniffed. A sweet smell he couldn't quite identify. He looked about at the newly grown meadow flowers that were scattered in the grass. They didn't seem to be the source.

Keeping to the edge of the trees, Power skirted round the long-lost lawns to get a better view of the Hall. As he got closer to the Hall he could see Michael's Land Rover parked near the old stable block.

The stable block had also benefited from re-investment and re-building. Perhaps this was where Michael lived. He wondered if both the McWilliam heirs lived at the Hall now and whether Lucinda lived in the Lodge, and Michael in the old stables, or vice versa. Power wondered whether the children had received insurance monies to enable the work. Lucinda had given him the impression that the deaths of her parents had left her impoverished.

Power sensed movement in the tableaux in front of him and ducked back into the shadow of the trees. He watched as Michael came out of the stables carrying what seemed to be a heavy bag of fertiliser. He hoisted the bag up onto his shoulder and walked across to a new, red steel door let into the gable end of the restored wing of the old Hall. As Power watched, Michael unlocked the red portal and entered. Power could hear the 'clang' of the door as Michael slammed it to behind himself. Power noticed, with some curiosity, that the door opened the wrong way. It opened outward.

He left the shadows and approached the door, intending to knock upon it and summon Michael from within. His actions were marked by ambitendence as he debated internally about why he had only just been hiding away so as not to be seen, and the contrast with announcing his presence by knocking on the door. Part of him wanted to find out why Michael had run from him. And another wanted to hide away. The very solid and fortified air of the red-steel door with bulbous, rounded rivets warned Power against knocking. This was no domestic restoration of Heaton Hall. This door was a fortification. He wondered now about how he might slink back into the shadows of the wood and whether he would be observed scurrying across the meadow-like grass to get there.

Power noticed that he was only feet away from the new conservatory. Huge vents were open in the gleaming side-walls and roof. The glass had been partially screened by blinds. He was afflicted by the same sickly sweet smell he had sensed before. Burning with curiosity, he edged over the side of the conservatory and bent over to look through a chink in the blinds to the room beyond.

Although there was daylight inside there were also strong lights in the furthest shadows on the conservatory. In the distance between the plants he could see Michael moving around, mixing up a solution of fertiliser in a big vat, fed by a hose. He dipped the watering can in whole and filled it up, wearing long rubber gloves, and began feeding the soil that the plants stood in.

Power gaped at the abundance of vegetation all around the inside of the house. The plants filled the conservatory, but inside the foil lined corridors and rooms beyond he could see a vast expanse of greenery continuing into the depths of the house, all under the brightest of lights. And the smell of the female plants was now heady and unambiguous. Power identified the spiky cannabis leaves at once. He was looking at the production of cannabis on an industrial scale.

All at once he heard the clanking of the gates at the end of the drive and watched the gates opening slowly and automatically. Power took to his heels and ran across to the trees, stumbling occasionally in the tangle of long grass and risking a headlong fall as he sprinted into the shadows, to turn and watch breathlessly as Lucinda's Porsche swung into the Hall's weed-strewn drive, and park as the gates closed to behind her.

She beeped her horn.

The new red door of the Hall swung open outwards, and Michael stood there, cigarette in hand, waving to her as she parked up and got out. Together they both went inside and the red door banged shut behind them.

* * *

Power did not sleep easily that night. His mind repeatedly reviewed his visit to Heaton Hall. His thoughts wound and re-wound like a film that played over and over from the moment he parked at Heaton and pushed his way though the lush undergrowth to the moment he ran back to his car and revved it away out of the lay-by.

He kept thinking about how both children had been there. How both of them must have been working on the old family estate and ploughing all their available funds into rebuilding the family home into a cannabis farm. He understood now the real reason why both Lucinda and Michael had run away when he had encountered them by chance. They were afraid of what he might do. They were afraid of his friend Lynch.

He slept badly.

From the early morning of the next day until evening, Power had dithered about what he should do next. Phone Lucinda and warn her that he knew everything? Phone Lynch and tell him about what he had seen? Or, prompted by some shred of loyalty to an ex-girlfriend to say nothing to anyone and thereby both jeopardise his friendship with Lynch and be complicit?

He felt anxious through the morning clinic and the afternoon ward round. He found he had lost his appetite for breakfast, lunch and tea.

On his return home that evening he sat in the lounge watching the national news on TV. Little of the events of the day in Parliament seemed to penetrate his confusion even when he turned the sound up. He felt he must do something, and suddenly stood up and made his way into the hallway where the telephone was. He picked up the phone's receiver and was poised to dial just as the national TV news switched to the local news and weather.

Words from the headlines of the local news bulletin drifted out from the lounge and punched their way into his consciousness. He watched the TV through the doorway in a state of morbid fascination.

"And in a secret early morning operation involving over a hundred police officers across Cheshire today, five cannabis farms were raided. The largest of these farms was at the ruins of Heaton Hall. Heaton Hall was burned down in a notorious fire some years ago. The fire claimed the life of Sir Ian McWilliam, the Cabinet Minister. Police found an extensive farm within the ground floor of the old Hall. Two people were arrested at the Hall, and nine others across Cheshire."

There were pictures of the Hall from earlier in the day. The bulletin included images of police milling around the red door where

Power himself had stood the day before.

The news bulletin moved on.

In something of a haze, Power dialled Lynch's number.

Lynch answered quickly.

"Andrew? It's Carl."

"Good evening, Carl. How are you?"

"I've just been watching the news," said Power. "About Heaton Hall."

"Ah," said Lynch. "Michael McWilliam and his sister. Yes, they've both been charged and are in custody. I'm not sure they'll get bail."

"When did you know?"

"For a while," said Lynch. "When we met for lunch I already knew. There was a meeting that very afternoon with the Chief to co-ordinate the operation. I didn't want to compromise you, so I couldn't say anything. Nothing in detail anyway. But then, by coincidence you'd seen her in town and you'd seen him that very morning. I am sorry if I seemed a little offhand with you. I felt I had to warn you – as strongly as I could – to stay clear. I have always tried to keep you clear of that two. The pair have always been, as the saying goes, as thick as thieves. They have both got first-rate minds, but wrongly focussed, wrongly employed. He's been running the farm and the distribution network. She's managed the books and investments. And they've also been part of something bigger across the County."

"You've known for a while?" Power felt slightly hurt that he'd not been entrusted with the information.

"I'm sorry, Carl. I really am. It wasn't because I had any worries about you. It was more to spare you the dilemma or the angst of what to do; avoid your worrying about her. You might care about her, even if she only cares for herself."

Power wondered if Lynch was being overly harsh about Lucinda.

On the other hand, he thought, both she and Michael had run from him . . . maybe Lynch was right and Lucinda really did not care about him.

Power realised that Lynch was still talking on the phone and listened with more attention, "I'm sorry, Carl, not to have brought you in on things. I do know you, you'd have made the right decision. Of course."

Lynch rang off shortly afterwards leaving Power wondering about things. What was the right decision? And Power realised that he still hadn't let his friend know about his visit to Heaton Hall the day before the raid. Although Lynch had been capable of keeping the Police operation to himself, Power had been equally capable of keeping his visit to the Hall a secret, and he realised he had no grounds for harbouring any resentment.

Power looked at himself in the hall mirror and felt slightly guilty about his friends. Then his stomach rumbled and he realised that he was overwhelmingly hungry and that the long fast that he had maintained through the day needed to be broken. He made his way into the kitchen.

The Fallen Man

June 16/17 1996

The Summons from Dublin was faxed to Dr Power on the Wednesday afternoon. He was not pleased to read the fax and scowled and growled at his secretary, Laura. "When did this come through? For God's sake!"

"Just now, Carl, I told you. Don't take it out on me." With that she exited his office to avoid any displaced wrath.

Power re-read the Summons again and phoned Laura. "I'm sorry to explode, but this Summons is for me to attend court on Friday. They've had the report for two whole years, and they contact me now! To get to Dublin for Friday!"

"You can do it," said Laura. "They have arranged a hotel for tomorrow night at least."

"I'll have to cancel everything," said Power.

Laura knew that this meant she would have to cancel everything.

"Please can you book me on a return flight?" asked Power. "Please?"

"If you pass your credit card through to me, I'll see what can be done. And I'll dig out a copy of the report – if you make me a cup of tea, either that, or I'm booking you on a one way flight."

"Okay," said Power. "I suppose it's a deal."

And so Power found himself strapped into flight EI3227 at 5.40 p.m. the next day. He clutched the arms of the seat anxiously at take off. There was barely time to read a chapter of a book before the plane was landing and taxi-ing to the terminal in Dublin.

The hotel Power had been booked into was near the Four Courts

Complex and clearly economy had been uppermost in the solicitor's mind. 'Functional', was the kindest word Power could think of for the concrete and steel hotel block. He checked in and stowed his meagre luggage. He had packed a fresh shirt, underclothes, sober tie, dark suit, copies of his notes and the report he had written on the patient. One look around the Identikit room was enough to convince Power he should go out immediately.

He crossed the River Liffey and climbed the street past the Cathedral and Castle to Wicklow Street. He paused at a cash machine to withdraw two hundred punts. Power's stomach growled at him, reminding him that he had chosen not to endure the dire airport cuisine.

Along Wicklow Street there was a red-painted restaurant called Cornucopia. The blackboard menu promised vegetarian and vegan food, and although Power hitherto had always loved his meat he ducked inside the front door as the place looked homely and friendly. The air inside was warm and welcoming.

A mainly female queue of people snaked its way to the counter. There were delicious smells of soup and beans, garlic and pasta, spice and oil, bread and apples. At the counter Power chose a chickpea and garlic parcel and a salad of cannelloni beans and aubergine. He bought a ginger juice drink and a strawberry shortbread to go with his main course and, tray laden, looked about to find a table. The doctor dithered as all around was a sea of occupied tables.

Standing forlornly with his full tray of food, Power suddenly saw a young girl waving to him from a table. She was smiling the broadest of smiles. Her face was round and she had deep brown eyes and long, tightly curled brown hair. She made eye contact with him and there seemed to be something, a spark of recognition maybe. Did he know her? How could he know her?

He threaded his way through the crowded tables towards her.

"Excuse me," he said, returning her smile. "Do I know you?"

"Not yet," she said. "Sit down, you look lost."

He put his food on the table. He noticed she was over halfway through her meal and thought she was maybe about to leave. "Thank you for letting me sit here," he said. "The place seems full."

"It's always full. There aren't too many places for vegetarians, as you know. Dublin is a great lover of the pig – bacon, sausage, black pudding – they love the pig. You aren't from around here."

"Is my English accent that obvious?"

"You have the air of being of other-worldly – I mean out of the Dublin world. My name is Penelope."

Power stretched out his hand. "I am Dr Power, faithful Penelope."

She giggled. "You know your myths, doctor."

"I have to," said Power. "It goes with being a psychiatrist. Oedipus, Electra . . . you know?"

"But what's your real name, Doctor? Your first name."

"Carl, Carl Power." And Power realised, all of a sudden, that he was smitten by her twinkling eyes. He felt almost embarrassed to eat in front of her, and struggled not to stare at her figure. He was conscious that he had blushed slightly.

"Well, there's nominative determinism. Being called Carl. A good name for a psychiatrist. Did your mother have a thing for Carl Jung?" She noticed that he wasn't eating. "Eat up, Carl. Or we'll be here all night." She patted his arm.

She told him that she was a postgraduate student. He thought she looked very young. She thought he looked distinguished in a scruffy, academic sort of way. She said she studied English. He said it was the right city and asked where. She said she studied and worked at Trinity College. Not far. And that she loved Dublin, although maybe her years here were coming to an end. Dublin had always welcomed outsiders, she said. Like Erwin Schrödinger, rescued by the Irish President from the claws of the Nazis. Maybe he should move here? The Irish were mad enough to need him. What was he doing here? The Four Courts had called him, he said. She understood. They couldn't stop talking. Power felt drunk on her presence.

Then their plates were empty and a drink was called for. She took him, her hand in his hand, down the way and left a bit to O'Neill's, where she clamoured for Guinness on their behalf and they stood, pressed close by the scrum of the crowd, waiting full two minutes while each pint of the black mild was drawn and settled and finished. And they looked into each others eyes and shared of their thoughts and feelings and conversation, while in the corner nearby, an old man, Vincent, fixed the couple with his ninety year old eyes, appraising the tall young man and the younger short girl with good thighs and breasts and all the attitude you'd want. Grinning and gurning, Vincent blew smoke rings up into the rafters of the pub and gave them his blessing. Power nodded to him and the old man winked craftily. They bought a second round and Power sent over another pint to the old boy. Then Penelope, student of English, spotted a mirror with Power's Irish Whiskey advertised thereupon, and the die was cast. Four double measures of Power's Whiskey were shared between them and consumed in a fashion and rate that the doctor was most unaccustomed to. He felt expanded, inflated, bigger than life and elated.

And so after O'Neill's, Power thought they were merely wandering through the Dublin streets, arm in arm, tipsy and benign, but Penny already had a destination in mind, and despite their apparently random course, joking and weaving their way, she led them ineluctably down Suffolk Street and on to the Lodge of Trinity College.

"You study here?" asked Power, admiring the classical white façade as she drew him through the bright archways of the Porter's Lodge.

"And work here," she waved a pass at the red-faced porter with his all-encompassing moustache. "Study and work, work and study . . ." she giggled.

"All work and no play makes Penny a dull girl," teased Power. She kissed him quickly, and before he could respond, as if to challenge the notion of dullness. They walked over the paved grounds inside the walls of the College, like twin chess pieces moving diagonally across a board. They skirted formal columned College buildings and walked over manicured lawns, past signs that promised daytime tourists coffee and sight of the Book of Kells. "I'd love to see the Book of Kells one day," he mused.

"There's not that much to see – a couple of pages from two of the Gospels under some glass. The exhibition before it is okay, with blown up images of symbols – peacocks and otters and fish – but the main thing on the tour is the Library, from King Charles' time – all wood and towering walls and walls of books."

"I'd like to see that," said Power.

"I was hoping you'd say that. See it you shall, Dr Power," said Penny. She was fiddling with the lock of a door.

"What are you doing, actually?" asked Power in a whisper.

"Opening up," she said. "Just a few hours earlier than I should be doing. I work here. I've got the keys and the alarm code." And with that she sneaked Power inside and locked the door behind them. They were both nervous and holding their breath in excitement.

"What are you doing?" asked Power.

"Entry through the gift shop," she said. Power looked around at the display stands burdened with twee tea towels, Celtic spiral jewelry and Trinity College Sweatshirts.

"It's just up here, up the stairs," she said, and led him by the hand as they ascended together out of the gift shop. She looked at her watch. It was past midnight. "The guards will have been round at 12. We have about two hours."

"What for?" asked Power, still whispering.

"You don't need to whisper," she said. "The guards go back to their concrete bunker and watch TV and drink whiskey. We've got the Long Room to ourselves. Exclusively." They had reached the top of the stairs and she spread her arms and turned slowly to show Power the Old Trinity College Library that filled the vast space above and around them both.

"Wow!" said Power. Although there was only limited light filtering in through the long windows on either side of the Long Room, Power could see a vast, round barrelled wooden ceiling, so high it was like the sky of this literary world. On every side were numerous alcoves on two levels, stretching away seemingly into infinity, each lined with leather bound tomes of every hue and tone. Each alcove was guarded by a bust of a notable person, set in two rows, each row of notables glaring at the other on the opposite side of the library. Power peered at some of their names in the gloom: Locke, Socrates, Newton, Johnson, Burke and Demosthenes.

Power turned to Penny. "We have two hours . . ." he said. ". . . two hours to do what? Rob the first edition of The Origin of Species?"

She came close, "No, silly." And she kissed him again, but this time lingeringly, and with her mouth opening unto him, hungrily. Power responded, suddenly overwhelmed with desire that had been building up all night. He felt himself hardening against her as she pushed herself against him. After a minute or so, Power surfaced for air.

"You had this planned," he said.

"Don't argue," she said, pulling at his trousers with deliberate

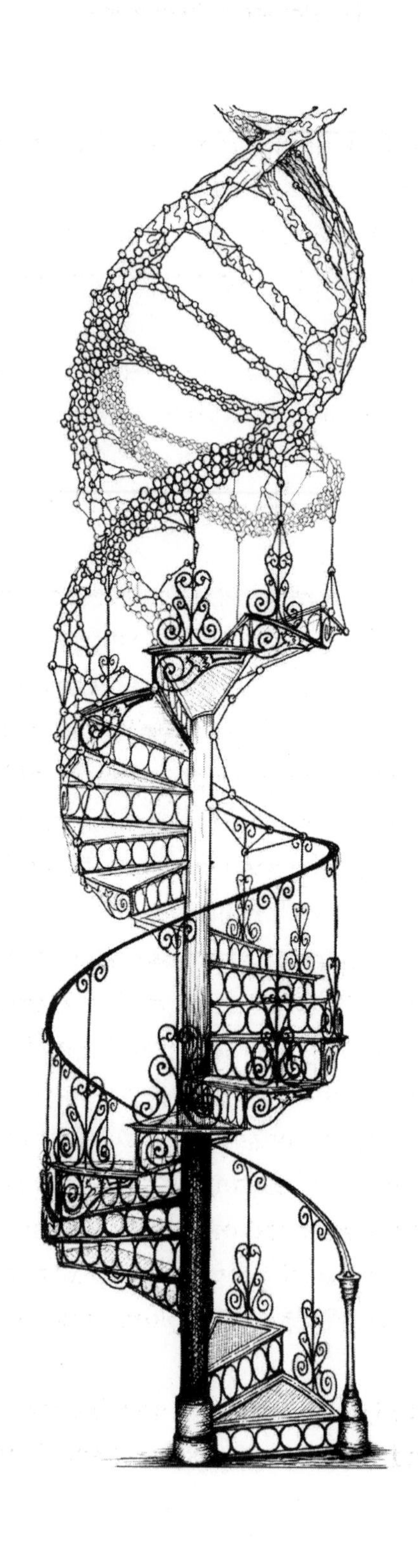

intent.

"I feel like King Charles is up in the balcony, or somebody else, watching us, looking down on us."

"In our fallen state? From what I know, King Charles would approve, for God's sake." His flies were opened and Power felt her reaching for him and building him up. "Down here," she insisted and drew him by the hand down the long gallery to a corner where Power glimpsed an elegant spiral staircase silhouetted against a long window.

"A stairal spirecase," he joked, as she simultaneously undressed him and herself.

Naked now, she climbed halfway up the staircase. She turned to him and beckoned. "Here," she demanded.

In the quiet velvet darkness of the Library and aroused to the point of uncomfortableness, Power followed her up the stairs. In the pattern of light and shade he caught glimpses of her large breasts, rounded buttocks and dark triangle of pubic hair. He placed a hand deliberately, cupping her between her legs and felt the springy wetness of her.

"Oh, God, yes," she said, as he opened her with his hand. Slowly she sat herself down on the filigreed metal stair treads, facing Power. She opened her thighs wide and invited him inside.

There on the stairs, sandwiched between two sheer walls of the world's greatest literature, Power and Penny combined and coupled, rode each other hungrily. Their mutual climax was swift, urgent and full. Penny's cries had bounced off the dusty book-lined walls and filled the sombre Library with more echoing ecstasy than it had seen in three hundred years. The books looked down, witnessing real life in the flesh.

Power panted and, spent, clung to her. She cradled his perspiring head with one hand and kissed his forehead fervently. Her other hand explored his back and haunches. "I love it when a plan comes together," she said. "I've been thinking of doing that for ever and ever. Since I first came to the University and tonight you made me dare . . . thank you." She looked at her watch. "We'd better go back to mine now. The guards will be round soon." They climbed down to their discarded piles of clothes and, cooling, they dressed and made their way to her study bedroom across the courtyards. Refreshed by the night air they undressed once more and, re-invigorated, Power was eager to consummate their passion once more. He watched her naked form as she lit candles and put on music. The flames gleamed deep in the pupils of her eyes as she pushed him back on the bed and straddling him, enclosed his gleeful tumescence within herself. Her face wore an expression of bliss as Penny took what she needed from Power.

Around 5 a.m. the first birdsong of the day accompanied the faint gleam of dawn over the College grounds. By now Power lay in slumber, his naked body half covered by a sheet. Penny watched his chest rising and falling as he breathed. She took in his handsome features in the warming morning light as he snored ever so gently on his back. She stroked his hair and his chest and smiled.

At 8 a.m. Power woke in a strange bed and felt disorientated. Scattered memories of the night assembled themselves and he smiled but also felt a wave of half-panic wash over him. What time was it? Was he late for Court? Where was he in Dublin in relation to the Court? His notes in the hotel – did he have time to get them? What had he done last night? Wasn't she too young? Had she really said she was a Postgraduate? Where were his clothes? How would he look in court without a suit and tie? Where was Penny anyway? Had he dreamt her?

Power called out her name twice, but the study bedroom was empty. Then he saw a note on the pile of his neatly folded clothes.

'Dear Carl, or should I say Dr Power?' Had she looked through his pockets? 'Thank you for last night and for fulfilling my Library fantasy! It was lovely. I've had to go to my tutorial. You will need to go to Court. Please phone me soon, Penny xxx' Penny had printed her mobile number at the bottom of the note. She'd also left out a tray with black Bewley's coffee, yoghurt and juice. Power smiled and breakfasted. He washed and dressed. Power was conscious of her perfume on his clothes as he gathered his few belongings. He went to the bathroom again to make water and was conscious, as he looked around, that he could see no pills of any kind amongst Penny's things. But he was anxious now about appearing in court and he hurried out of the student accommodation, across the courtyards, through the Porter's gate. He felt somewhat guilty under the gaze of the porters, but really they were unconcerned by the slim doctor as he rushed on by.

The Four Courts were across the River Liffey and Power ran through the streets to the Half-Penny Bridge. There was a breeze beginning to blow. The river looked high to him, or perhaps the other bridges along the river were too low. As he hurried, he started to wonder about Penny. Where did she come from? Was she English? Why hadn't he left a note for her? Should he phone her now, or later? He wondered again about whether he had merely dreamed the night before. The memories of the bar, the bewhiskered, bewhiskeyed old man laughing at them in their passion, the spiral Library staircase; all seemed too vivid and colourful to be true. As he scurried along the banks of the Liffey to the Courts he fumbled in his pocket and her note came to hand – he pulled it out and, pausing, looked at her handwriting – there was the proof of their night together.

As ill luck would have it the breeze picked up and a sudden gust plucked the note up from Power's grip and then cast it down. The note fluttered in its fall towards the green waters of the river. There was nothing to be done. It could never be retrieved. Power looked aghast for a moment until he remembered the Court and began to run again, cursing his luck and looking at his watch, he knew her name, her course, her College. He could find her again, surely. What was her surname though? Why hadn't he left her a note?

And then he was there, outside the security gate of the Four Courts. A short, misshapen man urged him to put any metal objects in a red plastic tray and herded him through a metal detector archway. Power complied, mindless with panic, and forgot to ask where the Court was. Although the complex was called the Four Courts there were more than thirty, as far as he could see, as he passed a few unhelpful signs in the vast courtyard.

He made his way as best he could to High Court 12. Power arrived perspiring after the run up the stairs. The corridor outside the Court where he was supposed to meet the Barrister was empty. Power paused at the door of Court 12 and listened. He could hear no sound, but the door looked stout and sturdy. He risked a glimpse inside. The Court was empty. A puzzled Dr Power made his way to a café in the centre of the complex. He followed signs, which led him into a dark lobby. A separate sign pointed to a Library, but declared 'Barristers Only', which excluded him immediately. He could see through an archway into the forbidden Shangri-la of books. A Dickensian scene of bespectacled men in black robes and white neckerchiefs poring over layers of books, with spines aligned and opened wide on green leather-topped tables. One looked up and glared through thick glass at Power, standing in the lobby in his stagnant shirtsleeves. Power ducked off to the left to be confronted by yet another sign that excluded him. Beyond a closed set of double doors Power could hear the clatter of breakfast things and smell the aroma of sausages and toast that wafted through the cracks at the edge of the doors. A stern, painted wooden sign pronounced

'Barristers' Dining Room. Barristers Only'. There was pompous laughter from within and the doctor felt small and unwanted. An ancient and typewritten, tattered paper sign said 'Public Café and Bar Downstairs'. At this point the carpeted floor gave way to cheap red linoleum as Power moved down the corridor to the stairs. He climbed down concrete steps.

Exiled to the depths of the building, Power nevertheless met with a warm enough welcome in the steamy basement café. He bought bottled water and a mug of steaming black coffee. He spoke to the cashier, "It's awfully quiet in the Court building. I was asked to be here for 9 a.m." She was a young woman in her twenties and her accent seemed to be Eastern European. She smiled, "Yes, they may be have a little joke with you. To get you here for sure, you know? The Judge start Court round 11, so barristers have breakfast first upstairs. Sausages. Bacon. Puddink. Toast. Guinness even. You see? And solicitors and witnesses they eat here." She waved her arm at the café tables where lesser beings like plaintiffs and solicitors sat amongst plates of processed pig – bacon, sausage, black pudding, white pudding and for variety an occasional egg amongst other plates with mounds of buttered toast. Power was not hungry. The witness box made him nervous.

He muttered a thank you for the information and sat down to wait. If Power had known he would have time, he would have written Penny a note, taken a taxi to the hotel, showered and changed into a sober suit and tie, and revised what he had written in his report. He was thirsty after the night's exertions and chugged down the water and then, more slowly, sipped the thin coffee.

Around 10.30 he essayed another visit to Court 12. The long corridor stretched emptily ahead of Power except for a small, squat figure in black sitting on a Spartan bench outside the court door. Power strode down the pink marbled linoleum floor and the barrister rose and presented him with a genuine smile. He extended a trembling, moist and plump handshake. His eyes were ever so slightly jaundiced and his skin was beset with a mildly lumpy complexion. "Sean Murphy," he said. "You are?"

"Dr Power," said Dr Power.

"Capital, take a seat. We've got a bit of time to chat until the Judge is here." He picked up a copy of Power's report and started reading it. "You saw Mr Fowler three years ago in England. And you describe the accident that Mr Fowler had on holiday in Ireland. He fell down the stairwell at the Bell Tower pub. Here in the city centre." The pub was in a converted church. "The guard rails on the stairs to and around the mezzanine were very low. You say he told you he lost his footing and went over and he landed in the stone crypt two storeys below. Of course, he is lucky to be alive and he knows it. You don't mention quite how the accident happens because he didn't know that – he didn't remember. He broke his back and shoulder and legs . . . he didn't tell you he was drunk did he?"

"Er . . . no," said Dr Power, instantly feeling guilty as if he should have known this. "He didn't mention that . . ."

"It doesn't matter Dr Power, for sure." Murphy patted Dr Power's shoulder. "It's just that the other side are fighting this tooth and nail, every inch of the way."

Power felt uneasy, a fight would mean a cross examination to within an inch of his life. He thought of his dishevelled state. "I'm sorry, I became detached from my suitcase. My suit was in it."

"No matter, Dr Power. It's a hot enough day." Indeed beads of perspiration were already evident on Murphy's brow, but Power wondered whether this was just because of the heat, or, alcohol withdrawal. "And as for Mr Fowler being drunk at the time of the fall – well it **was** a pub wasn't it? Where people drink and where the brewery should have taken account of this and made the stairs safe.

We've already called in an expert who has quoted the Council's own regulations for public stairwells in Dublin and that part of the case has been won, I think. Although you never can tell with his Lordship, the Judge, you know?" he looked down at Power's report again. "And you describe the psychiatric consequences of the fall. Mr Fowler has nightmares of the fall, and of being in the intensive care unit; he has flashbacks; he avoids heights and watching programmes with climbing or anything of the sort. And he's depressed because he's in chronic pain, and he can't go back to work as a plasterer because his shoulder doesn't move smoothly like it needs to any more. And you talk about his suicidal ideas. Now, on that point," he looked straight into Power's eyes. "Do you think he was trying to kill himself when he fell?'

"No, no," said Power. "He said he'd never been depressed before. And he was seen by Irish psychiatrists in the hospital after his fall and they excluded the possibility he was trying to kill himself."

"Of course, of course," Murphy smiled. "It would be a defence line of argument so I'm glad to hear you're so sure?" Power nodded. "Capital," said the Barrister. He stood up. Other people had been gathering about them. He looked down at Power. "Now, I'll be calling you after our orthopaedic expert. The Court's just finishing his cross examination. I need to warn you of one thing. Since you saw Mr Fowler, he has admitted, with much guilt and shame that he can drive a bit. They have video of him doing it, too. You'll know they often sit outside claimant's houses with the cameras."

Power nodded, he had watched hours of court surveillance videos, following claimants into restaurants or round supermarkets unbeknownst to them.

"Well anyway," said Murphy, "he admitted that the only reason he drives is to meet dealers who sell him cannabis, you know."

"For his pain?" asked Power. Such a thing was not unknown.

"Yes, he says he didn't mention the driving before though, because of the guilt."

"Well, it all fits," said Power. "Chronic pain and Post Traumatic Stress Disorder – I'm not surprised. 30% of people with PTSD misuse alcohol. 30% of people with alcohol dependence have PTSD. 8% of people with PTSD use cannabis or similar. To dampen down their distress. Blot it all out. It's a recognised feature of the illness."

Murphy nodded brightly. "Be sure to mention it, will you? The defence are making a meal of it and the Judge is set against cannabis. It's like a mission with him. It's illegal, that's all that matters to him and he's dead against it. If we can't argue it, then we'll lose the case." And with that, Murphy shook Power's hand and went down the corridor to another huddle of people, which had collected on another hard bench. Power was now surrounded by the chatter of both claimant and defendants teams. Mr Fowler sat glumly and silently at the end of the corridor in a wheelchair. He covered his eyes with his hands and appeared like he wanted to merge into the yellow walls, he gave every sign of wanting to be left strictly alone.

Power watched the clock tick its way to 11 a.m. and prepared himself for the Court, and then watched the clock tick on for ten, twenty and even thirty more minutes. At last the Judge was announced as having arrived in his rooms and the assembly was invited into the Court. The morning was nearly done.

They trooped into the Court. It was surprisingly cramped. Serried rows of benches, each higher than the preceding one ascended in a sort of stairway towards the empty Judge's bench. The emblem of Eire, a harp, hung over the Judge's seat. The boxes for witness and jury seemed to crowd in on either side. Power modestly took a seat on the rear bench of the main block, which gave him some sort of desk to rest some papers on, but was evicted by the Barristers' Juniors and relegated to the hardest of benches right at the rear against the bare wall where a few reporters sat. The plaintiff was wheeled alongside by a carer.

The ancient tortoise of an orthopaedic witness had taken his place in the witness box and looked over the assembled Court blinking feebly. 'It must be years since he operated on anybody,' thought Power, observing the man's hands and their tremor. 'At least I hope it's years since he operated.'

It was 11.40 when the Court stood up respectfully for the arrival of small, bewigged Judge Joyce. He nodded to the Court as they all nodded to him. His grey eyes glinted unfavourably over the assembled Court. "Please be seated," he said. He looked at the defence barrister, "I believe you were cross examining Mr Orpington, Mr Shaughnessy."

"Yes, My Lord," boomed the barrister and he turned to the witness. "Mr Orpington, may I remind you that you are still under oath." The surgeon inclined his head, ever so slowly. "May I remind you that you were describing the great difficulty that Mr Fowler had in transferring from his wheelchair to the examination couch in your consulting rooms? The difficulty was obvious I believe you said?"

"Yes," said Mr Orpington, his voice the whisper of dead dry leaves decaying under foot. "He was in great pain."

"I'm sorry," grated the Judge. "I cannot hear you. Move closer to the microphone, if you please."

With some difficulty, himself, Mr Orpington moved nearer the microphone. The stenographer, taking down the proceedings, regarded the surgeon through her glasses as if he were a fossil under a magnifying glass.

Power looked over at the long, casement windows. Outside, the Dublin sky was a deep deep blue. His stomach grumbled and he wondered whether he should have joined the solicitors at their breakfasts.

"Is that better?" croaked the surgeon into the microphone. The judge nodded with a semi-scowl, but Power could still hardly hear Mr Orpington.

"Well," said Shaughnessy refreshing his point. "You said he was in great pain. Have you seen the surveillance video?"

"Oh, yes," said the surgeon, seemingly innocently unaware of the serpent strike to come.

"And you saw Mr Fowler getting into the car and driving?"

"Yes."

"Did he tell you he could get into a car and drive?"

"No."

Feigned surprise from the barrister. "Did you even ask him?"

"I assumed that since he was on such a lot of pain medication that he wouldn't drive. I would have told him not to."

"With the greatest respect, Mr Orpington, that was not an answer to my question. If you have forgotten it, I asked whether you had asked Mr Fowler if he could drive?"

"No," said Mr Orpington.

"How do you explain it – how can a man who can hardly walk, hardly get on your examination couch, get into a car and drive it?"

"Pain causes different behaviours. I am a surgeon. I would defer to a psychiatrist. It is outside my field."

Power frowned. He hadn't been sent any video. Would he be asked to explain evidence he had never seen? He believed that Mr Orpington was dropping him in it.

Power was somewhat relieved that Mr Shaughnessy would not let Mr Orpington wriggle off the hook so conveniently. "You told the Court that you were an orthopaedic expert. You told the Court that you were a pain expert, that you had run a pain clinic . . ." Shaughnessy made a show of consulting his notes. "So surely pain behaviour is within your field of expertise?"

The tortoise-like surgeon suddenly rallied under the pressure. "The patient . . . Mr Fowler . . . was in great pain when I saw him. I believed him. People in pain will do anything to relieve their pain. I believe that he was driving to get some cannabis to help relieve his pain. He would have paid a price the next day for that activity – an increased level of pain."

Judge Joyce interrupted. "But I saw the video too, Mr Orpington, and everything you describe in your report – difficulty bending his legs, the difficulty moving his arms, difficulty picking things up, the difficulty moving, the pain in his face – all that you described, well that was NOT there in the video. I saw none of it. None at all. And I'm no medical expert. So how can you explain what I did not see in the footage?" the expert shrugged. The defence lawyer smiled smugly. "And all to go and get some drugs," grumbled the Judge. "Cannabis. Which. Is. Illegal." The defence lawyer reined in his broad smile. "Illegal," said the Judge more quietly and made a note to himself, as if this fact was something he had just discovered. Judge Joyce glared at the Court. "Any more questions from either of you?" He looked at both barristers. They shook their heads. The Judge looked at the clock. "Well, let's break for lunch. Be back at 2.00 p.m."

"All rise," said the Court usher, and they did as they were bade. And the Judge made a dignified exit for the Judges' dining room. The two barristers linked arms and left the Court chuckling, and went to the barrister's room for chops and a bottle of well-meant Claret. Mr Orpington was waved goodbye by the instructing solicitor.

Power went to the public café and munched on roast chicken, cabbage and chips. He watched the solicitors around him eating sandwiches and drinking chilled glasses containing pints of Pilsner lager and wondered how long the afternoon session would take. The morning's work in Court had lasted barely twenty minutes before lunch was called. Power fretted that his evidence would over-run to tomorrow. His flight was booked for that evening. He fell to thinking of Penny. He was still bemused at his behaviour. It wasn't like him to be so spontaneous. Had it all been a dream? The night before had assumed an oneiroid quality.

At 2 p.m. the Court re-convened and Mr Murphy invited Power to the stand to for his examination in chief. The Clerk of the Court told Power to take the New Testament in his hand and repeat the oath. A brief image of Superintendent Lynch praying in the Cathedral crossed Power's mind. He parroted the oath that he would tell the truth to the Court and was asked to sit down. A big bundle of the relevant evidence and reports sat in front of him. Power cautiously moved the microphone closer to him to avoid the spectacle of the deathly whispering of Orpington the Court had been given in the morning.

"Dr Power," said Mr Murphy, smiling reassuringly at him. "Tell us your qualifications."

"I'm a Consultant Psychiatrist in the NHS, practicing in general psychiatry. I'm qualified as a doctor – a Bachelor of Medicine and Surgery and a Member of the Royal College of Psychiatrists."

"Of course, of course," said Dr Murphy. "And you will see your report in the bundle in front of you at page 24. Now you saw Mr Fowler three years ago and you describe he said he lost his footing and fell backwards?"

"Yes, he told me that he was afraid he was going to die."

"To be sure, and I think that you outlined the psychiatric consequences?"

And Power described the clinical features that tortured Mr Fowler – the nightmares of falling that woke him in a panic, the anxieties during the day that something dreadful was just about to happen, the feeling of loss that he would never work again, the guilt at being a burden to his wife, how he couldn't bear closeness any more, and withdrew from everything because of the unremitting pain." Power sounded firm and assured.

"And what treatment did you recommend?"

"Different antidepressants from the ones he was taking, and psychotherapy."

"And he has had both," said Murphy. "But you were gloomy about his prognosis?"

"Because of his disabilities and his pain – whose mood can be fully recovered under those circumstances?"

The Judge interrupted, "And you haven't seen the video?"

"No, my Lord," said Power.

"Humph," said the Judge, unimpressed. "And what do you think of him taking cannabis? It is illegal in Ireland, you know."

"Well," said Power. "Cannabis is legitimately used in controlling chronic pain in some countries. There are various studies, which support its use in chronic pain. It is sometimes prescribed.

"It's also known that patients with PTSD also tend to use unofficial substances to control their symptoms. This is not supported by research, but it's a recognised feature of the illness – people blotting out their distress with alcohol or drugs like cannabis. 30% of people with PTSD use alcohol to excess. And 8% of people with PTSD use substances like cannabis. It's part and parcel of his illness, my Lord." Power conquered his fear of the Court and, to make his point, looked deep into the Judge's soul-less eyes.

The Judge broke eye contact first under Power's gaze. "Hmm, hmm," he said, making a note. "Any more questions, Mr Murphy?" Mr Murphy said he had finished. The Judge looked at Shaughnessy. Shaughnessy shook his head and avoided Power's eyes.

The Judge suddenly announced that the Court would rise for the day, stood and left in thoughtful silence.

Murphy sprang up and ran over to Power. "Thank you, thank

you, Dr Power. I think that all that's left now is a summing up from me and Mr Shaughnessy tomorrow morning, but that's the evidence complete."

"But, there were no questions from the defence," said Power. "I can go?"

"You can go. No questions – that's a good sign – he didn't want to give you the opportunity to carry on speaking. Any question he asked might let you say something that would undermine his case. No point in asking you anything, you see?" He shook Power's hand. "You were great. You were . . ." he sought for the right word. "Definitive! Definitive Dr Power."

And with that Dr Power left the Court and hailed a taxi to the hotel and then the airport.

By 5.20 p.m. Power was in the air. The sun glinted on his seat window as he stared down at Dublin city below. The city receded beneath him. As they climbed through the sky, through the clouds that had appeared out of the blue, the city disappeared.

Dr Power thought through the events of the day and allowed himself a quiet smile. "Definitive," he mused.

Magpies
March 1997

Seated at his oak desk in his study Dr Power was trying his very best to focus on a research paper that he was writing. However, he was being easily distracted. The tall window in front of him offered a view into the woods round Alderley House. There were two magpies strutting on the grass, foraging for insects and pulling on worms that had surfaced after the rain.

Power's mind ran through the nursery rhyme over and over: 'One for sorrow, Two for joy, Three for a girl, Four for a boy, Five for silver, Six for gold, Seven for a secret, Never to be told'. Power had never been superstitious, and would protest that he was a sceptic in practically all matters, but still part of him was pleased that he could see two magpies. All of a sudden there was a startling flurry of feathers and the birds ascended in panic as a silver black tabby cat bounded and pounced on the spot where they had been. As he watched, both magpies flew up into the lower branches of one of his garden's oak trees.

The cat sat back on its haunches and looked up at the branches of the trees where the magpies had landed. The two species regarded each other with mutual hatred. The staring contest went on for a long time and then the cat's head swivelled as it looked directly at Power. 'Maybe he senses my gaze,' wondered Power. Power looked momentarily at the computer screen on his desk and when he looked through the window again, the cat was gone.

He tried to re-focus on the paper he was writing about traumatic grief. It was proving difficult to complete. He watched the blinking

cursor and tried to form a sentence in his mind that he could set down. At the side of the document window another was open. He had been looking at a webpage that featured an old program that had been written in the 1960s and which mimicked a therapist working in the style of Dr Carl Rogers. Dr Power had an empathy with this often forgotten therapist, because he shared the same first name. Rogerian therapy included the notion that the therapist should show 'unconditional positive regard' for the patient, and be non-judgmental.

He started the on-line therapy program up and the virtual therapist said, "Hello".

"Good morning," typed Power. It was only 9 o'clock but Power had been working for a few hours on this Saturday morning to try and finish his writing. His stomach rumbled. He was thinking of breakfast.

"Don't you ever say hello?"

"Hello," said Power.

"How are you? What would you like to discuss?"

"My lack of coffee," wrote Power.

"Can you elaborate on that?" asked the therapist.

"I've run out of ground coffee, and instant coffee, and coffee beans," wrote Power, which was true. He had used the last granules up after dinner the night before.

"Why don't you know what to do?"

"Maybe I should drive down the hill and go and get some?"

"Can't you be more positive?"

"All right," said Power. I WILL go and get some."

"Now that is interesting!" said the therapist/server, which was sitting in the basement of a University, many thousands of miles away.

With this virtual endorsement of his plan, Power logged off and went upstairs to get showered and dressed.

The sun was shining somewhat feebly from behind grey clouds as he unlocked the Saab and got in. The drive down the hill to the village and along Alderley Road to Wilmslow took him maybe quarter of an hour. He parked near the supermarket and, fetching a basket, began questing the aisles for ground coffee and a jar of good Instant.

Power was brought to a sudden halt in one of the aisles by the sight of an older woman in a once-good coat holding two tins as she inspected and compared their silvered ends, all the while muttering to herself. As he drew near, Power could hear her mumbling numbers or some form of a calculation.

Power drew alongside her. Her head was bowed and she was intent on her inner world. "Hello, can I help?" he offered.

She looked up, expecting to see a uniformed shop assistant. Instead she saw the soft velvet jacketed figure of Dr Carl Power, psychiatrist. "You interrupted me," she chided him. "I'll have to start again."

"What are you doing? Can I help?" he asked again.

She handed Power the tins of soup and took off her glasses and regarded him. "I know it might sound odd, but I am checking the numbers on the bottom of the tins."

"To make sure they are in date?" Power looked at the bottom of the tin at the date and serial number of the batch which was printed there.

"No, no, no." She frowned, realizing she would have to try and formulate some kind of answer that made sense. "It has to be the right number. They have to make the right number."

"I'm not sure that I follow you," said Dr Power.

"I didn't think you would understand," she said. "Sometimes I add them together. Sometimes I subtract them. Sometimes I multiply certain ones. But the answer has to be the right one in the end."

"Like magpies?"

She looked at Power as if he were mad. "As long as the number is not thirty, I can buy the tin."

"And if the number is thirty?"

"It goes back on the shelf, for somebody else. So you see, you interrupted me while I was calculating."

Power looked at the numbers. "I can't make thirty out of these numbers if I add or subtract them."

"Today is a multiplication day," she said. "That takes longer." She took the tins from him again and scanned the bottom, then put the tins back on the shelf.

"Wrong number?" asked Power.

"No, I've gone off the idea of soup." And with that she moved off down the aisle with her small trolley load of groceries towards the checkouts. Power was left behind to assemble his own wire basket of coffee, pain au raisin, and fresh fruit. He looked at the delicatessen counter and wondered about going into the city for his evening meal.

When Power had paid for his two small bags of shopping he noticed the old woman again. This time she was at the customer service desk and arguing about her bill. Power wondered if he was being too nosey, but he wandered over anyway, wondering again if he could help. The old lady was trying to return an item from her shopping. She caught sight of Power and waved him over. "Look," she jabbed a finger at the receipt. He took it from her and looked at the total. "I chose it all carefully to avoid this. I paid for it using my card, and when I checked, it was wrong." The total was £30.

"I'm sorry, madam," the customer service manager was saying.

"No, it's wrong. It's £30."

Power scrutinised the bill. "I think I see," he said to the old lady. "You chose your shopping carefully and added the prices of the items to avoid the number thirty. But there was a discount applied by the computer that nudged the total down to exactly £30."

"Exactly," said the old lady, "It's wrong."

The blonde shop worker was exasperated. "No, it's right, the bill's right. We've taken money off your bill."

Power interceded. "You're correct, the bill is correct, but for this particular customer the total is wrong. Wrong for her. Perhaps," he turned to the old lady. "Perhaps you could exchange an item for a refund, that would change the total, or donate a small amount . . . maybe donate the discount you earned to charity? Then the total you've paid would not be £30?"

The old lady smiled, "Of course, what a sensible young man." She put the £1 she had earned in discount into a charity box for Asperger's syndrome standing on the counter. "Do you know, you remind me of someone I once knew. He didn't look like you, but he was so, so clever."

The customer service assistant smiled. Dr Power had defused the situation. Power took the white-haired old lady's arm, "Shall we have a cup of tea or something?" He nodded at the road outside the store's front window – to the café across the road – and as they both carried their shopping Power guided her there. He ordered a tray of tea and some jam and scones.

They took a seat near the café window. Outside, on the road, Power's classic Saab shone in the sunlight. Power offered her his hand, "I'm Dr Power, glad to meet you."

She smiled, "I'm Eliza, Eliza Clayton." She shook his hand.

"Shall I pour?" asked Dr Power, as he picked up the steel teapot.

She nodded. "Thank you for helping me out."

"Do you live in Wilmslow?"

"Mount Pleasant. A terraced cottage, I've lived there for years. You wouldn't believe the changes in the area. My cottage is small, but we couldn't begin to afford to buy it nowadays. The prices have gone up so much, with all these posh people moving in." She giggled. "They're not really posh though. They've got money but no manners. Not a gentleman, like you."

"Forgive me for asking," said Power. "Have you always had a dislike of the number thirty?"

"For many years. Over thirty years," she joked. "Since the 1950s. A very long time ago for you. You weren't even born then, I dare say. I've had a thing about thirty ever since I worked for Mr T at Hollymeade in Adlington Road. I was his cleaner." She frowned and looked out of the window, pausing. Power knew that he should not interrupt these pauses. "He left me £30 in his Will, Mr T did. And £10 a year for every year of service." She fixed Power's brown eyes with her own watery blue gaze. "It felt like thirty pieces of silver, Dr Power. Not that I sold him to anyone. I just felt I'd let him down, somehow. They did try to talk to me. The men in the car who I caught watching his house asked me questions, and the reporters after he died, of course. But I wouldn't say anything. It would have been . . . unethical. Against my code. He was a man who liked numbers. Loved them. They were . . . almost everything to him." She sighed. "I sometimes look at the numbers. Look for meanings in things. Like he might leave a message for me in them. I know it's silly of me. How could he? He's long dead and gone. Dust now, probably."

"Why do you think you let him down then?"

Eliza took a sip of tea, and buttered a scone. "Because I sometimes think I could have done something. If I'd noticed, maybe. Maybe I could have helped him. But I looked after him. I was a widow in those days. Not long been a widow, and he was so vulnerable. He needed my help. He was always so . . . dishevelled. I tried my best, but he'd wear any old thing. A bit too involved in his work. His numbers. He thought they governed everything. How plants grew.

How snails built their shells. How leopards got their spots." She laughed. "He'd try and explain things – his experiments and his counting machines. It was all important hush hush stuff. It was the Cold War then. He'd have his papers and bits and pieces strewn everywhere. Parts from early computers, all from Ferranti in Cheadle. That's a firm that's gone now. Killed off by the Americans, I heard.

"Well, I cleaned for him four days a week – Monday, Tuesday, Thursday and Friday. 4 o'clock sharp to 8 o'clock sharp. I couldn't have done those hours if my Jack had been alive, of course. Jack would have wanted his own tea on the table in the evening. But I was Mr T's housekeeper in the Fifties, and when he got home from the University where he worked I'd have tea ready for him. Mutton chops were his favourite. He asked for those the night before he died. I did his shopping you see, and I always made his evening meal."

"How did your employer die?" asked Power. "How do you think that you could possibly have prevented it?" There was a long pause and Power could see that Eliza's eyes were full of tears. He noticed her cup was dry and the tea-pot was empty. "Let me order some more tea." He signalled over to the waitress.

"It's difficult for me," she said. "I'm sure you can see that. After he died I had to attend the Inquest. And it took years for the dreams to go away. It was like being haunted.

"The Inquest finding was that he killed himself," she said this starkly, as a matter of fact. "Using cyanide. I found him. The day after, when I came round to start work. I was a bit later than normal, but it didn't matter I suppose. He'd gone the night before. I could see his bedroom light was on. He never drew the curtains. And there he was in the front bedroom, dead. And cold. The room smelt of almonds. He was in bed, under the covers with the sheets up to his neck. His mouth was covered in a kind of froth." She shuddered.

"Who was he? Mr T? What was his full name?"

"I called him Mr T. His first name was Alan, but I wouldn't call him that. He was Mr T or Sir. He was quite famous. He was Mr Turing. He lived here in Wilmslow."

"Ah," said Power, some realisation dawning upon him, at last. "Alan Turing. I didn't know he lived near here. He was the codebreaker in the war, wasn't he."

"Yes, but he was more than that, I think," said Eliza. "He thought that one day computers would have intelligence, and he saw maths everywhere, in everything. He was so young when he died, and what more could he have discovered? He was a 'quair fellow' though. That's what we would have called him when I was a girl. He didn't fit in. His neighbour, Mr Gibson, said he dressed like a tramp. He'd wear a gas mask in the summer to guard against hayfever. He stammered occasionally when he was excited or nervous. He was easily embarrassed and rather shy. And of course, he was what we used to call a confirmed bachelor."

"You mean he was gay?"

"If that's what they call it today. It never bothered me, although Mr Gibson asked me how I could ever work there. I told him that everyone deserves love. He looked at me as if I was from another planet. But that's how things were in those days. Do you know how old I am, Dr Power?"

"I couldn't possibly say," said Power, smiling.

"I'm ninety-two. So I'm very, very old and I've come to know how very different everyone is. No two people are the same. So we have to be tolerant. He had his friends, but he was considerate and polite and he wasn't the kind of person who'd ever embarrass you with any shenanigans with boys or girls. But they wouldn't let him be. He was prosecuted for being with one young man. And they made him see a psychiatrist and take pills that made him sick. His psychiatrist was Dr Grunbaum. I met him." Power felt uncomfortable. He hadn't introduced himself as a psychiatrist and wondered what she might say. He was aware of how psychologists in the 1950s had treated 'deviants'. One of his patients had told him of aversion therapy where he was shown a series of pictures and how his genitals were electrocuted in synchrony with any slides of a homoerotic nature. "Dr Grunbaum was a psychiatrist, a proper good doctor," she went on. "But he didn't try and cure Mr T. He was interested in his dreams and made Mr T keep books of his dreams. Every dream he remembered in the morning, Mr T would write it down to discuss with Dr Grunbaum."

"I was worried you were going to say something bad about Dr Grunbaum," said Power. "I should confess that I'm a psychiatrist too."

She fixed Dr Power with her twinkling blue eyes and smiled. "I thought so," she said. "Dr Grunbaum told me that he was an analyst that had escaped from the Germans and that he had trained with someone famous."

"Sigmund Freud?" She shook her head.

"Adler? Jung?"

"That one, Jung. That was the one." She sipped her third cup of tea thoughtfully. "Dr Grunbaum was very surprised that Alan killed himself. He hadn't imagined that would happen. And if his doctor was surprised . . ."

"Did you imagine it would happen?"

She shook her head. "I never saw him depressed. He was never ill. Apart from hayfever. He was occasionally angry. He had a friend, Kjell, coming to stay once. From Norway. He'd sent a postcard, which they read. When Alan got the postcard he was very enthusiastic and looking forward to seeing his friend. But they must have been reading his post. And his friend never came. That made Alan angry."

"He'd done such secret work for the security services, did they maybe think Alan was a security risk?"

"How would I know?" she said. "I was just a cleaner. In the newspaper cuttings I kept, they name everybody who gave evidence. Me? I was just 'the cleaner'. Not even a housekeeper. I wasn't given a name. Not that I'd want the publicity, I suppose, but it sort of hurt me."

"Do you think you could have stopped his suicide?"

"Oh dear, you haven't been listening. I have never thought it was suicide. I always worried that I could have prevented his death. Stopped it happening."

"I'm sorry, I didn't understand. Tell me what you mean, please?"

"Mr T brought his work home with him. He had a lab in the back bedroom. Electrics and solutions. Plating things like spoons with gold and studying the maths behind it. Who knows what it was all about? But that's where the cyanide came in. He always told me never to clean in there. He did that. To protect me."

"You think it was an accident then? That he accidentally poisoned himself?"

"His mother thought that, I know. She preferred that idea to suicide. I'm not so sure, but I don't think it was suicide."

"Why?"

"He was a polite man, and a considerate man. I believe that he liked me. Why would he eat a dish of my mutton chops and then go and poison himself that evening for me to find the next day. For me to find him. He wouldn't do it. He was too polite, too considerate. That and there was no poison."

"So if I'm right, you believe that he wouldn't have wished to upset you by killing himself and leaving his body for you to find."

"That's what I thought, and I told them that at the time when they were investigating his death but they weren't interested in my opinion. 'Keep to the facts' the policeman said when he was taking my statement. But I know that Alan wouldn't have wished that sight upon me. You are a proper doctor aren't you?"

Power nodded. "I've served my time as a House Physician and a House Surgeon and I was also a Registrar in Chest Medicine once upon a time."

"Then can I ask you something? If someone drank cyanide . . . how quickly would they die?"

Power frowned. "It would be very quick. Seconds. Convulsions in less than a minute, then the breathing would stop. A few minutes before the heart stopped."

"I thought so," she went quiet. "Convulsions?"

"Violent convulsions. Writhing about."

"I see. There was no glass in his room. There was a half eaten apple on the bedside table. He liked an apple before bed. He always did. But they didn't test that. They found cyanide solution in his stomach. There was cyanide in the house for his experiments, but that was in the other room. A way off. There was no glass of poison on his table, or in the bedroom where he was found.

"And you think . . . ?"

"Well, you say that Mr T would have died within seconds of drinking anything?"

"Yes."

"I can't work it out, you see. The poison was in another room. If he drank it, he drank it there. Although, I don't think he did. If he drank it there, do you follow . . . did he have time? He was in his pyjamas. Who gets dressed for bed before they kill themselves, in any case? He would have had to drink the poison in one room. He would have had to place the poison down and then he would have had to run through to the other room, get into bed, lie down and pull the clothes up to his neck. Can you do all that in a few seconds before you die? Do you think? And why would you do that? Why would you take poison and then quickly run to another room and lie down in bed? After all these years it is a puzzle that torments me. I can't make sense of it and I know I never will now. Not at my age."

Power shook his head. She was right. It did not make sense. "And he was *under* the sheets? Up to his neck?"

"Pulled up to his neck."

"And you were the first to find him?"

"I found him like that, and I went to the neighbours. At once. To phone the police." She could see that Power was puzzled. "What are you thinking?"

"I am thinking that cyanide would cause convulsions. Agitated writhing. I'm sorry, this must be distressing," Power was realising that she had experienced all this. She'd lived through it, and been haunted by it for decades. "The point I am trying to make is that if he had had convulsions, on the bed . . . he would have moved about, contorted himself. And yet, you described before, that the sheets were pulled up . . . to his neck. My question is, how?"

There was a silence. The old lady poured a last cup of tea for them both.

"Quite," she nodded. "And yet that was how he was. How I found him. How I saw it, with my own eyes."

"And you think that . . . ?"

"I think that I could have saved him," she burst into tears and felt for his hand. He was so wrapped up in his world. He couldn't see the danger. I'd seen them outside watching his house from the car. I'd point them out to Alan and do you know what he said? He called them 'poor sweeties' – he was sorry for them having to sit outside in all weathers. He didn't see the danger."

"What could you have done?"

"Something, something. Called the police. I don't know. Got him to move. I don't know."

"You wanted to protect him?"

"Of course."

"I'm sure you did everything you could," said Power.

"It never feels like that; I feel guilty."

"And that's why you check the numbers. To undo what has been done?"

She sobbed very quietly, almost keening. Power reached out his hand and held her small, thin fingers. After a while, her sobs became less frequent and she pulled her hand away to reach into her pocket for a soft, white handkerchief. She dabbed at her eyes, and smiled at Power. "It was all a long time ago, Dr Power. More than fifty years. It sometimes feels like yesterday, but you know, I've never told anybody all the things I've told you today. Thank you for listening. Do you think I'll ever know what really happened? I've lived with this guilt all these years."

"You were a good friend to him," said Power. "I'm sure you did everything possible." (Later, when Power related the account to Andrew Lynch and asked for his thoughts, Lynch had murmured about her being a 'good friend and a faithful servant', but he would not be drawn into making any promise to look into the case).

"I feel better for meeting you, Dr Power," Eliza said as she slowly stood up. "Oooh, I've got stiff knees."

"Would you like a lift?" he offered.

"Thank you, that's kind, but I'll walk the stiffness off, if you don't mind," she said. "I didn't get to ninety-two by being lazy." She picked her shopping up. "You know, maybe I will stop checking the numbers on the tins now. I've done it too long, perhaps. Time to let it go. Well goodbye, Dr Power." She shook his hand and he watched her leave the café.

After settling their bill, Power gathered his own shopping and drove back down the road and up the hill to Alderley House. He

ELIZA
JOSEPH
WEIZENBAUM
CHESTE

ground some coffee beans. He poured the grounds with their heavenly aroma into a cafetiere and poured in boiling water. He carried the cafetiere and his favourite mug into the study and sat down at his desk. From the window he could now see a scattered group of magpies. Automatically, a slave to the superstitious rhyme, Power counted them. Five. Five for silver. He thought back to the old lady and wondered whether she would ever stop looking for the numbers on tins and cease trying to divine the number thirty in the midst of the numbers on the base of the tin. His conversation with the old lady had given him some new ideas. He switched the computer back on, and the last browser window flickered back up. It was the computer therapist program. He typed in:

"Thank you for talking to me before. What do you think of counting magpies as a pastime?"

The computer replied, "We were discussing you, not me."

"I got the coffee."

"Come, come, elucidate your thoughts," said the program/therapist.

"I met Eliza."

"Tell me more . . ."

It was at this point that Power noticed, for the first time that the program had a name. At the bottom of the screen he read that the program had been devised in 1966 by Joseph Weizenbaum.

The program's name was Eliza.

The Unmother
April 1997

Dr Power was lying back in his armchair in his office staring at the ceiling. On the table by his hand was a stack of square crisp white paper. He was listening to Elgar's variations and folding piece after piece into small paper aircraft, which he threw into the lofty space above his head and watched them as they flew across the room towards the door.

All at once the door to his office opened. The planes that had gathered on the floor were shoved unceremoniously to one side and his secretary, Laura, stood there. She put her hands on her hips, snorted and frowned at her Consultant.

"You look gorgeous when you are angry," said Dr Power, appeasingly.

"You're meant to be dictating discharge letters, Carl."

"Must I? Can't Rachel do that?" Rachel was Carl's junior doctor.

"Have you been on the lazy pills, Dr Power? And you know very well that she's not been in post long enough." She turned on her heel. "And turn off that music when you are dictating. I don't want that miserable classical music on the tape when I'm trying to decipher what you are saying."

"That is the Enigma Variations!"

Her blue eyes flashed. "It sounds more like the Enema variations to me."

Power slung the whole pile of paper at her quickly retreating figure. By now she had closed the door, however, and the sheets of paper cascaded over the carpeted floor. He sighed, and got up to start picking the paper up. He was just switching the CD player off to begin dictating when Laura stuck her head around the door again. She lurked defensively on one side of the door. Power suddenly thought how very pretty she was, and this thought drowned out whatever she had started saying.

"I'm sorry," he said. "Please could you repeat that?"

"There's been a phone call from Court. And you are the consultant on take this week. The Judge is asking whether you will accept a patient for a report under Section 35. Will you phone the female secure unit? They need your report that aids the Judge in sentencing . . . you know?"

Power was grateful for Laura's reminder as to what Section 35 entailed. To be honest he found anything beyond one or two of the main sections of the Mental Health Act very confusing.

"Okay, I will phone the ward manager."

Power sat down behind his desk and phoned the female secure unit. Sarah, the ward manager, answered. "Hello, Carl. Thanks for phoning back. The Court in Chester have been on. Judge Gregson would like you to take in a woman on remand for a report. Apparently the Judge was told that the accused said she wanted to hang herself and he'd like a report on her before he goes any further."

"Judge Gregson?"

"That's what the court clerk said."

"Judge Gregson is a she, not a he. I've given evidence before her in the past."

"I stand corrected," said Sarah. "Well this woman on remand is a twenty-two year old who's charged with serious long term neglect to a child under the Children and Young Persons Act. The Court wants to know if she's mad or bad. Can you agree to provide them with a report."

"How long have I got to assess her?"

"Four weeks. That's the standard. Can be extended to 12 weeks, but four is the usual, Carl. Will you take her?"

"The case sounds interesting, yes."

"Interesting? It sounds distressing, that's what it sounds like, Carl. Still that's the bread and butter of what we do, isn't it?"

The patient arrived from custody the very next day and, as promised, Dr Power walked, shivering, across the hospital grounds, over tarmac and closely trimmed lawns, to the secure unit. The rain spattered over his broad shoulders. The uncertain weather meant he was in the sudden midst of a Spring shower and yet despite the rain the sun was also shining into his eyes and the falling water droplets glistened like diamonds all about him as they fell to rest on the green grass.

He arrived at a squat brick building, which sat partially encompassed by an 18-foot high concrete wall, which surrounded the ward garden and prevented escape. A bulbous and protruding metal cap ran round the top to prevent any attempt by a patient to scale the wall.

Power buzzed his way into the ward airlock and waited just beyond the first set of doors for a nurse to escort him past the second door, with its Home Office specification locks, onto the female secure ward.

Deon, a nurse from St. Lucia, took the doctor onto the ward. There was a distant wolf whistle from one of the patients as Power walked through the dining area. He tried his best to ignore the collective gaze of the patients at the tables. There was a babble of various voices calling out and barracking him; "Are you seeing me today, Doctor?", "When can I go home, Doctor?" and "Can you take me to bed, Doctor?" None of these people were his patients. He recalled how he used to be embarrassed at the calls and whistles that inevitably met his entry onto the secure wards.

The nurse in charge, whom Power respectfully referred to as Sister, although this term was now becoming clouded with sexist tones, was called Sarah. She was pouring out a cup of tea as Power closed the ward office door behind himself. "Would you like one?"

"Yes, please."

Sarah poured out a steaming mug full of tea and nodded towards a file on the desk. "Those are her notes. Nothing in them yet. Some court papers relating to her section, not much more. Are you happy to see Sharon before, or after your junior?"

Power took a glug of tea. "I'll take the first history," he said. Power liked to take a good history – he found it was the only way to get to know the patient. "I'll leave the examination to my junior, though. Will you come in with me while I see Sharon?" Power never saw patients on the secure wards on his own, for safety's sake. Sarah nodded. "What's your first impression?"

"She's quiet, Carl. And she's a pretty girl. Tall. Well dressed. Looks a bit shocked to be here, to be honest. Not what she was expecting perhaps? I have asked the ward staff not to say too much about her to any patients. I mean, we don't reveal any details anyway, but to be especially careful. And I think maybe we shouldn't even say much about her to the staff . . ."

"Why?" asked Power.

"You might find that attitudes to her change, or harden if what she's accused of becomes known."

"I'd hope we can rise above that, as professionals," said Power. Sarah fixed him with a look . "I'm sorry," he said. "Was I sounding a bit pompous?"

"Just a bit, Carl. And I know you're right, we should be detached. We shouldn't judge. But that professional veneer often evaporates when a child is involved. I've been warned that the statements and police evidence is . . . upsetting."

"Well," said Dr Power. "Let's focus on looking after her, and observing for any signs of mental illness." Power recalled a ward he'd been on as a trainee in a secure hospital where the bitter old charge nurse kept his alternative and informal patient records. He had once shown them to Power. Tiny, well-thumbed record cards kept in an old tobacco tin. Each card had the name of a patient on the ward, and a single sentence detailing their worst crime. The nurse had told Power – 'That's all you need to know. What they're in for. That's what you keep in your mind – what they would do again, if they weren't under lock and key.'

"You'll have to look at the witness statements about Sharon some time, if you're writing the report," warned Sarah.

Power nodded, "You're right, of course. It's just that the crimes sometimes cloud your perception of the individual. Shall we see her?"

Sister Sarah had put the patient in an interview room, sitting with a staff nurse, separate from the other patients. The staff nurse was taking some details and orientating her to the ward routine. When Power walked in the patient, Sharon, began sniffing and gently sobbing into a handkerchief. He noticed her soft perfume, long shiny chestnut hair and devastatingly handsome hazel eyes. She smiled, albeit wanly, at him. Her lips were full and rounded.

Power sat down and the staff nurse made her excuses and let Sister take her place. Power coughed nervously all of a sudden, found himself a blank sheet of paper in the notes, and took out his black Lamy fountain pen. Sarah watched him, amused at his response to the girl, and pondered how Power's little homily about the need for objectivity seemed to have dissolved on his sight of Sharon.

"Sharon, I'm Dr Power." Power held out a hand and she shook it. Her handshake was surprisingly firm and dry. "I am your Consultant."

"Are you writing the report?" It was an unusual first question.

"Yes," said Dr Power. "Why?"

"Nothing," she smiled at him, and sniffed. Sarah handed her a box of tissues.

"How are you?" asked Power.

"Dreadfully down. I can't begin to tell you. Ever since . . . . Ever since they took him away from me and put me in a prison cell." She began sobbing again.

"How old are you, Sharon?"

"Twenty-two."

"Where do you live? What do you do?"

"I live in Blacon, and work as a barmaid in a pub in town, The 'Oak Barrel'. Do you know it? If you call in you can have a drink on the house." She actually fluttered her eyelashes and smiled at Power and he sat back at the sudden transition from sadness to flirting. But just as suddenly her eyes were downcast and she was glum again. Maybe she had registered Power's surprise.

"A barmaid?" asked Power. "That's a job with difficult hours to fit round childcare. You just have the one child? Never any others?"

"Just the one, my son Kyle. He's two." Power made a note.

"How did you manage his childcare while you were working?"

"Oh, my stepmother would help out. Or neighbours. There was never any problem."

"Uhuh," said Power. "And what do you think about the social services and what they've done?"

"You mean taking Kyle into foster care?"

"Yes, and your prosecution?" Power wondered if he was asking the question too early, whether she would find it easier to just clam up.

"It's so unfair. I miss him so much," and this cued another bout of tears. Sharon grabbed a fistful of tissues from the proffered box. Power somehow got the feeling that Sharon's tears were purely for herself.

"How will he feel?" asked Power.

Sharon looked a bit surprised and had to give the matter some thought. The fact that she paused made Power's heart sink. "I suppose he'll be lonely, she said.

"What's your sleeping like?"

"All right," she said. "Where I live, the flat, is noisy so even in a place like this I sleep better. And there are less interruptions."

"You mean from Kyle?"

She burst into tears again.

And so Power took his history and learned that Sharon had been born in North Wales near a caravan park. Her parents had divorced when she was ten and she'd lived with her mother, who had found it difficult to cope with her, she said. She had truanted from school and there had been conflict over her attendance. Her favourite subject had been Art. She'd spent nights with her school friend whose family had owned a caravan park and eventually Sharon had moved in to the park from the age of fourteen. Her father had moved to Spain and run a pub called Eastenders then come back onto the scene after he had re-married and moved back to Wales to look after his ageing parents. She had been asked, she said, to move in with Dad and his new wife in a village called Elton. When she was nineteen her parents had helped her get a flat in Blacon, she said this was to be nearer the city for her. Blacon was a rough area where the local police station had the appearance of being fortified against native resistance. She had been lonely, and fallen in love with a boy who lived with her for a few weeks, before travelling down south. She had become pregnant with Kyle, and the rest was history. Power asked probe questions about episodes of depression in her teens, alcohol misuse, drugs, overdoses, deliberate self-harm, bulimic binges, baby blues and postnatal depression. She regarded him playfully as he asked, and yielded up a few clues. She had been very down after Kyle's birth, lonely, starved of sleep, had struggled to breast feed the child, lost weight. Maybe drunk a bit too much? And Power dutifully wrote it all down, and wondered whether it was true.

He left her in the capable hands of Sarah and her nurses and asked them to make contact with any relative of Sharon's who might be willing to come and see him. A few days later Laura showed Sharon's stepmother, Diane, into Power's office and he took a collateral history. He started to notice discrepancies with Sharon's version almost at once. Her stepmother was a solid woman dressed in black. She spoke without smiling and her voice was ringingly clear. She had first met Sharon when she was sixteen. Diane had just married Sharon's father, Derek, in a small civil wedding service in the seaside town of Rhyl. Sharon had not been invited, as she was out of contact with her family. They had found her living in a dilapidated caravan near the shore. She was drinking and smoking cannabis. Her habit was fuelled by money and bottles of vodka from the men who visited the caravan from the town at night. Her father had been horrified and had gathered her to him and railed at his ex-wife at her abandonment of Sharon. Sharon had painted a bleak picture of a cruel biological mother, his ex-wife, that he had believed. Sharon had reportedly been starved by her mother both of food and of affection and had only survived through the kindness of the parents of school friends. All had gone well with the re-united family, and the move to Elton had gone well. And then there had been a few episodes where Sharon had stayed out all night and there were reports of her sleeping with men in the village. Her father had been upset.

Diane had taken it upon herself to drive to North Wales to talk to the family of the friends Sharon said she had lived with. They said they had put her up for a few nights, but they had found her a bad influence. Drugs were found in her bed. Sharon had been cast out. Then she visited Sharon's mother. And she heard another story. Sharon had been an absent child from the age of fourteen; she had spent time hanging round the pizza and kebab shops. Her mother couldn't control her. She would be gone for whole weekends and her mother found the police of little help. The police said it was 'a lifestyle choice'. Social services had been critical of the mother and her parenting and so mother felt undermined and unsupported. Sharon had sworn at her, punched her, and one evening pushed her downstairs. She had hit her head on the bannisters as she hurtled down the stairs, and lain there stunned at the bottom of the stairs as Sharon stepped over her and went through the front door to her lovers, uncaring of whether her mother was alive or dead. Her mother had given up after that, fearing for her life and bemused by her daughter's callousness.

Diane had watched Sharon's father struggle to look after his daughter and guide her. Diane had never seen Sharon show any other person genuine affection. After supporting her for three years her father had reluctantly encouraged her to get her own flat and job. Sharon had fallen pregnant shortly after that.

"Did the pregnancy change her? Did she become maternal?" asked Power.

"I think she fell pregnant to try and keep her boyfriend, but he was colder than her, and he left. That wasn't in her plan. Her father was upset that she fell pregnant and that she was alone. He talked about having her back home, and I supported him. I said yes, but I was worried. In the event Sharon didn't want to move back home. I think she was frightened of the supervision. I spoke to the neighbours and they described parties, and callers at all times of day and night. I didn't tell her father. There is only so much you men can be told. He was delighted when he held the baby, and for a few weeks everything was fantastic. I spoke to her. She promised to mend her ways and she came back to us. But it wasn't long. A month or so, maybe. She was glued to her phone, and giggling and laughing on the phone to her boyfriends. And there were the requests for us to babysit. Her father was in a haze or something. He was besotted with Kyle. And then he noticed too; she'd stay out all night and he realised we were being used. There was a big row. He insisted on closer supervision and that if she was in his house she must stick to his rules. Well, she is too headstrong to be treated like that. Her mother had tried all that."

"So she left?" asked Power.

"Back to her flat. She hadn't got rid of that. And of course Derek was distraught. He felt so guilty and tried to get her back. But she wouldn't answer her mobile to him, or act on the messages he left. Then he became worried about the boy. I became worried about Kyle too. He was such a cute baby. But months went past. Then she responded to a card her father sent her in the Summer. She responded a few weeks before her birthday. And we visited her in a café. It was good to see the baby was Okay. Well we thought he was okay. He was dressed up in a big all-in one suit. And it was summer. He must have been hot. But he didn't seem distressed. He didn't smile or anything really. But we were so glad to see her. She said she was working part-time in a café and that she had a childminder. Her father said he'd mind the boy, but she laughed at him. And she took her birthday present. Derek had put together a few hundred for her. And she left. Just like that. And we didn't hear of her again for a few months, until just before Christmas. And we went through the same routine again. The café. The present. And Kyle was in this big suit thing. He didn't look much bigger, and he didn't make a sound. Derek wanted to pick him up and cuddle him. But she made some excuse. I can't believe we didn't pick him up and run."

"So what happened next?" said Power as he looked up from his notes.

"I went round to the flat one evening, to try and talk to her, to try and see Kyle. She was out. I couldn't hear anything through the flat door. I assumed that she was out somewhere with the boy. I knocked on the neighbours' doors. They didn't seem reliable people. One was drunk. The others had needlemarks on their arms, but they were sober. They said that Sharon worked as a barmaid in a club in the evenings. And that she slept during the day. They never saw her with an infant. They never even heard an infant." She was tapping her hand on the Power's desk in agitation. "I tracked her down a week later in a club and I confronted her. She had an answer for everything. The baby was being looked after by a friend she had at the club. They took it in turns to work and look after each other's children. That was the story. But I didn't believe her. I thought about going to the social services then. I should have done. But how would I have explained that to her father? If I'd been wrong? I waited until Easter and the same performance. The usual meeting in a café. This time I planned things and I forewarned my doctor about what I might do. She warned me not to do what I planned and suggested other methods. But I knew my plan would work. I planned it. I visited the café beforehand to plan my route. I sent her a card from her father and me, suggesting a meal at the usual café at the usual time. Well she turned up with Kyle expecting the usual present. And I went in. On my own. Her father knew nothing about it. I told her that her father was outside – that he had had to stay outside because he'd bought a new car for her and that she was to go out. I'd stay with Kyle. She believed me, because I'd never lied to her before. And as soon as she gone out the café front door I picked Kyle up and I ran out the back door. I'd left my car there, with a babyseat in it. And I drove so fast. I was shaking. I drove to my GP, and I said –'There he is. I brought him. Check him.' There was a protest, of course. Something about not wanting to be an accessory to abduction, but I stood my ground and I insisted. And the GP examined Kyle in front of me." She paused, and Power could see tears welling up in her eyes.

"You were brave, taking him there."

"I only wish I'd done it sooner," she sobbed for a moment. "The GP, she took off his padded suit and underneath he was naked,apart from this sodden nappy, and so, so pale. No underclothes. And he was . . . thin . . . emaciated. You could see his ribs. And he was covered in scabs and bruises. He had scratched himself because he had mites. The GP . . . she gasped, and she took photographs. And I cuddled the boy in a blanket while she called social services and the police. It was so awful. Like a nightmare. I felt frightened and guilty and embarrassed. They kept telling me I'd done the right thing. But I felt awful."

"Where is Kyle now?" asked Power.

"With foster carers," she said. "But Derek and I, we hope that after all this, the Court case, we hope we can be his carers, adopt him."

Power nodded. "And what happened with Sharon? Once she learned about Kyle being taken into care."

"After I left. After I'd taken Kyle to the doctor . . . you might think she'd be distressed. Maybe that she'd call the police and report me. She disappeared. There was a warrant for her arrest. When the police went round to her flat she wasn't there. She'd gone out clubbing. They found her after she'd been out paralytic on the pavement outside a club at 2 a.m. What do you think of that?"

"No remorse?" asked Power. Sharon's stepmother shook her head. Power sighed.

"You should see the photos of her flat. Where she kept him. She used to leave him alone in there. For hours and hours and hours.

Days sometimes, I think."

Power didn't want to see any photographs. Part of him still wanted to believe that there was a chance that illness might explain Sharon's behaviour. Wanted to believe that illness, rather than Sharon, was responsible for Kyle's plight.

"Kyle isn't the same. When he was little, he used to smile. He doesn't smile now. He doesn't try to talk, he doesn't make any noise. Like he's given up. Do you think he's . . . damaged."

Power was downcast, "That relationship with the mother . . . the to and fro of emotion and expression . . . the talking . . . the nurturing . . . the smiles . . . the reassurance and holding . . . it gives you your sense of self, your resilience. I don't know what to say. Maybe if Kyle can bond again with you and his grandfather . . ." But Power knew that so much had been lost, and how the developing child's brain relies upon that relationship with its adult carer.

Later that evening, at home, Lynch rang. After some light conversation Lynch asked Power about the case. Sitting in his hall, by the telephone, clutching a glass of Pilsner, Power was loathe to dwell any more on the case. His response to Lynch's enquiry was noticeably curt and sought to curtail any discussion, Lynch picked up his friend's reluctance.

"I know it's a bad case," Lynch said. "Upsetting. And I'm sorry to intrude. Sergeant Beresford told me that the detective who is making the prosecution case offered to show you the photos of the flat and the child. Beresford said that you didn't want to see them."

"That's right," snapped Power. "I don't want my judgment of the case altered. I'm trying to focus just on her symptoms. Just on whether any illness is present."

"I understand," said Lynch. "I understand you. You don't want to think badly of your patient." Power stayed silent. Lynch had got it absolutely right. "You don't want to judge her. But you need to know. And you will be shown the exhibits in court. Best to be prepared, don't you think?"

"The police want a conviction. You want a conviction. And you don't want me going all touchy-feely and wishy-washy and liberal."

Lynch sighed. He had seen the photographs, and yes, he did want a conviction. Part of him burned with anger at what the unmother had done. He wondered whether he should quote Isaiah 49:15, and decided that Power was in no fit state to be preached at. "I just want you to see things how they are," said Lynch. "Sometimes you try so hard to see the good in everyone, Carl. The detective will be coming to the hospital again tomorrow. Take a look at the pictures. If you can, please." And with that the two friends said goodnight.

* * *

He saw the female detective at 10 a.m. Power had not slept well the night before and Laura had made him a couple of strong coffees, which she watched him pour down his throat before the detective arrived. The detective tried to engage Power in small talk and asked how Sharon was, but Power regarded her sullenly. "If I must look at these photos, please can we look at them and get it over with?" he said.

"They're pretty bad," she said handing them to Power. "But not as bad as the smell in the flat. She hadn't emptied the bins for weeks. And they were full of used nappies." She wrinkled her nose. Power looked at the photos of the living room. Bare lino on the floor. A battered leather sofa, with tears or cut marks where the stuffing oozed out. A trail of swollen nappies lay on the floor, where they had fallen off the child as it walked or crawled around. Photos in the kitchen showed an absence of food in the cupboards, a few boxes of cereals lay on the kitchen floor where the child had eaten from them. "We believe, from statements, that the child was left alone, with the music turned up. For up to two days on his own."

"Didn't the neighbours hear his crying?"

"I think he'd given up," she said.

"But what did he do for drinks? Did she leave him drinks, water? The sink would be too high." He was anxious about her response. Power wondered with revulsion about the toilet bowl.

"She put a stool by the bath. He'd climb in there to drink out of the tap."

Power looked at the photos of the bathroom. The stool by the bath. The old nappies strewn around. He imagined the silent lonely hours of the infant, wandering about the flat; abandoned, hungry, and thirsty. He felt sick. "You wouldn't keep a dog like this." He felt tears prickle the back of his eyes and struggled to maintain some form of composure. He thrust the photos back at the police officer. "I've seen enough," he said.

"You haven't seen the medical photographer's work. They took proper photos of the boy in hospital."

"I've seen enough," said Power. "You've done what you needed to do. You wanted to convince me about her. You can go."

The detective gathered the photos together and put them safely away, stood up, stiffly wished him goodbye, and left. Power sat in silence for a while.

* * *

Power suddenly shrugged off his fit of despondency. He felt he must exorcise the case from his mind by completing his report. He needed now to gather the nurses' observations of their patient. His initial working diagnosis had been depression. But depression, clinical depression, is a persistent thing that cannot be lifted by pleasant circumstance, a shadow that endures, clouding everything. Objective records of sleep, and appetite and behaviour were required.

Galvanised by his urgent need to put the case behind him, Power ran down the stairs and out of the building, across the lawns to the secure ward. Sarah, the ward manager, met him from the airlock and walked with him down the corridor.

"Another visitor for Sharon! Isn't she popular? I hear you met the police officer and saw the photos."

Power grimaced. "Are there other visitors?"

Sarah smiled and silently beckoned Power towards the door leading into the visitors' suite. He looked through the glass window in the door. There were three people inside. A nurse in the corner, observing interactions and chaperoning. She would have previously searched Sharon's visitors and any belongings. It wasn't unusual for visitors to try and smuggle drugs onto the ward – heroin in a mobile phone case, amphetamines in the bottom of a cylinder of Pringle's crisps.

Power moved his head to see where Sharon was. She was sitting on the knee of a young man and her arms were round his neck. Sharon was oblivious of Power's gaze. Occasionally she would kiss her visitor's cheek quickly and laugh. He was boy in his late teens, in t-shirt and skinny blue jeans, thin-faced and stubbled. The nurse in the room looked uncomfortable.

Power looked at Sarah and frowned. She whispered so that she wasn't overhead, "Don't worry, Carl. We won't let anything happen . . . but I do want to see what she does. How far she will push it. One thing we've learned is we don't think there's anything wrong with her libido. She's been begging boyo there to visit for days."

"Who is he?"

"Someone she met in passing in the police station while she was being charged. An unsuspecting member of the general public who she passed her details to. I tell you this, Carl, she's a fast worker. No man is safe. Even our gay nursing assistants have been subjected to non-stop flirtation."

Power's frown became a glower of annoyance. "And her sleep? How does she sleep at night?"

"Like a top."

"And her appetite? He qualified this, "For food?"

"No problems."

Power shook his head. "Can I see her please? Just for ten minutes? If you can interrupt her? She should be able to go back in a moment . . ." Sara nodded as Power went and unlocked the interview room for himself.

Sarah brought the patient in a few minutes later. She sat down by the interview desk near Power. Her posture and behaviour seemed to be that of another person entirely to the vivacious young girl he had just observed in the visitors' room.

"Good morning, Sharon," he said. She didn't look at him, but fixed her downcast gaze on the floor. She mumbled a low hello and looked sullen and sad.

"How are you?" he asked.

"What do you expect?"

"I'm not sure. I've come to see how you are. Can you tell me?"

"Have you finished my report?"

"Not quite," said Power. "Which is why I've come to see how you are? How are you feeling?"

"I miss him so, I can't stop thinking about Kyle and where he is. I can't sleep at night. I just wonder where he is. When will I be able to see him again, Doctor?"

"I don't know," said Power. He was struggling not to say something else. "It must be difficult for you?"

"Terrible, you can't know what it is to be separated from your child."

"How low do you feel?"

"The lowest I've ever felt. If they don't give him back to me . . . life is not worth living."

"The thing I'm struggling with," said Power. "Is when did all this low mood start? I mean, some psychiatrists would say that maybe you are saying you are down because you are frightened what will happen to you? And others might say something different, what do you think?"

"I've been down since Kyle was born. I've never been right. It's post-natal." She looked at Power to try and gauge what he thought – whether he was agreeing with this line of defence. "The other doctor thought so, and he's a Professor."

Power was perplexed. "Professor?"

"I'm sorry, Carl," said Sister Sarah. "I didn't have time to tell you. Sharon's defence team have asked for their own court report. Professor Anastasi has been on the ward all morning. He's in the office reading Sharon's notes."

"Anastasi!" Power spluttered in distaste. He had had the misfortune to write expert court reports in the same cases as Anastasi before. Power felt his heart sink. Anastasi always took an opposing stance, and the Court saw him as a charming, senior and consummate professional. Power loathed him, although he would concede that his loathing was possibly irrational and instinctive.

"You know him?" asked Sharon. "What's wrong with him?"

"Nothing, nothing," said Power, struggling to regain his professional composure. "Well, that was all I wanted to ask. I can let you get back to your visitor. Do you know him well?"

She looked up at him warily, "Were you watching us?"

Power stood up. "Thanks for talking to me," and he opened the door. Sarah escorted Sharon back to the visitors' room and Power wondered what to do next.

He decided that a conversation with Anastasi was unavoidable.

He left the interview, carefully locking the door behind him, and made his way down the corridor to the ward office. As he expected, Anastasi was sitting at a desk in the corner, reading through Sharon's case file and making his own notes. As Power unlocked the door and entered, Anastasi looked up. He was a small man with closely cropped black hair, and piercing brown eyes. He wore gold-rimmed, half-moon reading glasses attached to a cord. He slipped the glasses off his long, thin nose and stood up. "Professor Power!" he exclaimed and advanced on Power with a smile, extending his palm for a handshake.

Power shook his hand. Although Anastasi's hand was small he had a dry and vice-like grip. "I am Dr Power," he corrected Anastasi. "Not a Professor."

"It is merely a matter of time," said Anastasi grinning. "I tease you, maybe? But you will be a Professor, I am sure of it. I am reading your notes. Insightful, yes."

"You met Sharon?"

"Yes, yes." Anastasi sat down and put his spectacles on to make his final notes. "She is very depressed? No?"

"No," said Power. She's not depressed at all."

"But yes," said Anastasi. "What mother treats her child so neglectfully unless she is mad?" He wagged his finger at Power. "You have recorded what she says. She said the same to me and she was so despondent when I interviewed her."

"An act," said Dr Power.

"She describes symptoms of depression since the child was born. Clearly post-natal depression. Anyway, you are her treating consultant. You of all people should be more . . . sympathetic. You are writing a report, too?"

"Yes, yes," said Power. "But you need to take into account the nursing observations, the history of her stepmother."

"What do nurses know?" snapped Anastasi, irritably. "They are not trained in diagnosis! And since when has a stepmother ever liked their stepchild? She won't be saying anything to help her . . ." He stood up and his anger seemed to evaporate as quickly as it had boiled up. He clapped Power on the shoulder. "Bear my words in mind . . . you will be a Professor. I am sure!"

And with that Professor Anastasi gathered up his notes and breezed out of the ward office.

* * *

Lynch placed a pint of bitter in front of a glum-faced Dr Power. "Cheer up," he said, as he sat down opposite the doctor at the beer garden table. He looked about him at the pub's rolling lawns and the fields beyond, which were golden in the setting summer sun. "You can't win them all, and you have to realise that on this earth of ours justice is imperfect."

"But the Judge clearly preferred Anastasi's report," said Power. It had been a fortnight since the trial and his professional pride had not yet recovered. "He's the hired gun amongst psychiatric experts, the most venal . . ." Power sipped his beer. His stomach rumbled and he wondered whether the kitchen was still open.

"He's a Professor," said Lynch. "It sounds impressive to the Court. Sometimes it's not the quality of the argument."

"It shouldn't be like that. It's the truth that matters. And the truth was that it wasn't a psychiatric illness that led to the boy's neglect. Anastasi didn't bother to ask the nurses for their observations. They never saw any signs of depression. Her stepmother described clear features of sociopathy and no sign of illness. And the pictures . . . I bet he never saw the photographs of the child or that terrible, terrible flat."

"There was a conviction," said Lynch, trying to pacify his friend.

"A community order with a condition she attends for treatment with a psychologist."

Power snorted in derision. "Where's the justice in that? The child will never recover – he's been robbed of so much . . . so much development at a crucial, crucial time."

"It's not every time you get the conviction and the sentence you want as a police officer," said Lynch. "Sometimes we just have to wait for Divine justice. Do you remember the verse in the Bible? 'But whoso shall offend one of these little ones which believe in me, it were better for him that a millstone were hanged about his neck, and that he were drowned in the depth of the sea.'"

"That's all very well," said Power. "But the last I heard was the nurses had seen her when they were out in Chester at Brannigans at the weekend. She was there, partying with her new boyfriend, till dawn. I wish Anastasi could have seen her."

"At least her son is away from her now and safe," said Lynch.

Power nodded in a resigned fashion. "My concern is with the son."

"Me too," said Lynch.

Christmas 1997

Flying in the face of all that seems fair and right, Christmas does not dispel or suspend a person's susceptibility to illness.

There is no sentimental truce between the forces of health and life, and the forces of entropy and death.

And so it was that Dr Power found himself working late on Christmas Eve, battling the demons that beset one of his oldest patients.

Mary Stone lay mute and uncomprehending, her very being plunged into the pit of depression. Her thin grey hair was uncombed and smeared onto her damp forehead. She lay on the trolley, her gaze fixed straight ahead on the ceiling. Her thin body shivered involuntarily within the equally thin cotton ward nightdress and Power sought a blanket and threw it over her. "Not long Mary, you'll soon feel better."

He turned to the girl beside him. She was Lynch's niece, Sam, a prospective medical student. Power had been showing her the hospital and his work all week, with the hope that this experience would count towards her medical school application.

"Mary is usually a very chatty lady," said Power. "I know she won't mind me saying that, will you, Mary?" Power looked at the deathly still patient by his side. She stared ahead, giving no sign that she had heard him. A flicker of concern crossed his face. "But Mary is very different today. Her GP found her at home yesterday. She hasn't been eating, or drinking. Power gently pinched the skin on the back of Mary's hand. The pinched skin remained as a thin ridge after he took his hand away, and only gradually subsided back down.

"She's very dehydrated, so I've put a drip up," he said. "Real medicine for once."

Power nodded to the ward nurse standing at the head of the patient's trolley. "We'll be back when the anaesthetist arrives," he said, and he drew Sam over to a desk in the room behind. "Take a seat, and I'll tell you about Mary."

Sam seated herself, and asked, "Is she dying?"

"Not today if we can help it," said Power. "But if we did nothing, then yes . . . she would die."

"But she's so still, so thin."

"Yes," said Power. "As it is, she is dying. She isn't eating or drinking. Her electrolytes are deranged. If we left her, then her kidneys would fail, or she'd get pneumonia. She has been neglecting herself for weeks. This is severe depression."

"Surely people don't die of depression!"

Power nodded. "Yes, they do. And today, I hope, we will save her life. I've known Mary for many years. She seems to find me wherever I am. I knew her when I worked at the Royal in Liverpool, and then in North Cheshire, and now they've sent her from the NHS to this hospital because there are no beds at her home hospital."

"No room at the Inn", said Sam.

"Irony," said Power. "Yes, no room. For someone as ill as Mary. It sometimes feels like the magic is wearing very thin." Sam frowned and wondered what he meant. He was off on another track now though. "Mary was a downtrodden housewife when I first knew her. I think she was regularly beaten up by her husband on a Saturday night, but she was always too proud, or afraid to say. I'd probe to find out, but she never said. Then when the children were grown up. When they had flown the nest, she packed her bags, and she flew too. That took courage. Huge courage."

"Why?"

"Well, firstly, courage to defy that man, and then courage to set off, to set course and voyage into uncertainty, with no home and no money. She did well for a while and then she became depressed again. She has recurrent depression and she becomes very low. And that was when I first knew her. She had ECT – electroconvulsive therapy."

"How barbaric!"

Power looked a little uncomfortable. "What do you mean?" he asked.

"Frying people's brains."

"Erm, that's a popular misconception. Do you know how much electrical energy is used? You do physics at school? How many megavolts or whatever do you think we use?"

Sam thought for a moment. "I don't know . . . at 13 amps, several joules of energy? A few coulombs?"

"No, it would be 700 mC. Millicoulombs, a tiny fraction of what you said. The electricity is a very small amount and pulsed to cause a fit, an epileptic fit, which is modified by a muscle relaxant . . . so you don't even see it . . . it's just inside the brain, and limited to less than thirty seconds. Small amounts of energy, a small fit. Maybe you'd just see some flickering of the lips, a slight twitch of the fingers."

"I heard it causes brain damage."

"No," said Power. "There are some reports of memory problems, but these are usually transitory. Not remembering the day before, say. But then depression causes people not to be able to concentrate, so they can't form memories anyway, and the alternative, leaving the patient as they are – not treating them – is not so good. Because make no mistake about it, if we don't do something, then Mary will simply fade away."

"What about antidepressants?"

Well, Mary is usually on those, and also on a mood stabilizer, but she forgets to take them, or stops taking them. And slowly at first, she declines and relapses. We will re-start her medicines, but they will take a month or so to work. We can't wait that long, Mary doesn't have that time." He paused. "She's had several courses of ECT over the years, and I want to give her some tonight. I've asked the anaesthetist in to help."

"Anaesthetist?"

"The ECT only takes a few seconds, but we give a sedative, a short acting general anaesthetic and a muscle relaxant. If we didn't give the muscle relaxant Mary would have a big fit, a grand mal fit. That was the kind of ECT they did in the 1930s. This is streamlined stuff. You can watch if you like?"

Sam shuddered. "I don't know."

"If you don't see, you'll never know. If you watch and see Mary before and after – that's the only way I will convince you that this works. And there are people who are closing ECT down. It's illegal in several places in the world."

"Maybe that's the way forward," said Sam. "What if you are wrong."

"And if I'm right? And we lose another piece of magic? Will we go back to how things were? There was a German psychiatrist called Emil Kraepelin. He did work studying how long mental illness lasts. He worked before we had effective drugs, before ECT. In those days if you had schizophrenia you might easily go into hospital for twenty years or more and never come out. I know you might have been sad in the past." Power knew that Sam's father had died a few years before. "But imagine that sadness, bad as it was, even worse and never getting better. Kraepelin described patients with depression lasting ten years or longer. What wouldn't you do to try and relieve their suffering? I remember reading about a case. A case of a man in England, at a Victorian asylum called Ticehurst,who had depression.

Depression so bad that he was deluded. He thought that there was no future. That even his head and stomach did not exist. He believed that so strongly that he stopped eating. Why eat, he reasoned, if you have no head and no stomach. And he felt this way for ten years."

Sam looked sceptical. "If he didn't eat for ten years. How did he survive?"

"They fed him. They passed a nasogastric tube. Three times a day. And they poured beef tea and olive oil down the pipe to give him his food. A liquid diet. And in that way they kept him alive, just. And that's what psychiatry would be like, without our antidepressants and our ECT."

"Well, we have talking therapies now, things have moved on."

"But, before the 1930s, before ECT, we had Freud and the talking therapies. He was writing his works in the 1890s. We had hypnotism. There were talking therapies in the old asylum in Baghdad hundreds of years ago. We've been able to talk to one another forever. And still we've had mental illness. So I'm sad that people are forgetting how it was. It's like being a wizard with no magic." Sam looked pale and unconvinced. "Go and talk to Mary. See what you think of her now, before the treatment."

"I don't know what to say," said Sam.

Power nodded. Sometimes even medical students didn't know what to say to psychiatric patients, and Sam was still at school. "Just say hello, introduce yourself, try and engage her in conversation, about anything at all, anything you can – the weather, the news – anything. Ask her a question – is she warm? Does she have enough pillows? Anything you like."

Sam walked over to the trolley with some reluctance. The nurse at the head of Mary's bed looked at her quizzically. Sam saw no hint of reassurance there. She looked back at Power for support, but he was checking through some forms. She looked down at the patient.

She stood close to her side, but Mary did not acknowledge she was there and stared into some intermediate space above the trolley. Mary was so still and her chest was moving up and down so gradually that Sam wondered if she was still alive. Mary's breath smelled sweet, like fruit. "Mary?" asked Sam. "Can I talk to you?" Silence. "My name is Sam. I'm working with Dr Power. How long have you known him? Can I ask you some questions?" There was no response and Sam felt a wave of panic and the hairs on the back of her neck rose. She fumbled back in her memory to Power's suggestions for conversation. "Are you comfortable, Mary? Can I get you anything? A drink?"

The nurse was the only one to respond and to Sam's discomfiture shook her head at the suggestion of a drink for Mary. "Another pillow then?" There was no sign that Mary had heard or seen Sam, and feeling defeated Sam retreated to the side room where Dr Power waited.

"I couldn't get any response, nothing," said Sam. "It was frightening."

"No," said Power. "Mary is in a severe depressive stupor. People talk about psychomotor slowing or psychomotor retardation. Basically everything has slowed down. Little movement, and thoughts stuck like cold treacle. An emptiness, or wasteland of thought, profound despair. This is illness – and it is a killer."

The clinic door opened and in breezed the anaesthetic registrar. She was pretty, young and petite. Her brown eyes twinkled healthily in the clinic lights that had been switched on as the afternoon dusk fell. When Power stood up to greet her he towered above her. "Dr Potts," she shook his hand vigorously. "Christmas Eve – what kind of time is this to summon me from the general?" But her manner was teasing and she seemed pleased to be there.

"It's Mary, again," said Power. She needs the first treatment of a new course."

"I know her, said Dr Potts. "I looked after her in Spring during her last course. "I've re-read her notes too. Any medical updates for me? Any new illnesses? Any recent chest infections?"

"No," said Power. "I put up an isotonic drip. Her urea and electrolytes were all to pot. She's not been drinking." He gestured to Sam. "We've got an observer, a candidate for medical school. Do you mind if she watches?"

Dr Potts nodded to Sam. "Do you want to put the electrodes on?" Sam shook her head vigorously, and Potts laughed. "It's not going to hurt! And you can say you've saved a life!"

"Maybe not today," said Power, "Sam doesn't want any blame attaching to her," said Power, "and I don't think she's convinced it will help, yet. Shall we get on?"

But Dr Potts had already started laying out the syringes and drugs she needed from the bag she had brought. She checked the clinic oxygen supply, the mask, the bag and the tubing. She was swift but methodical. Power mirrored her activity and switched on and checked the ECT machine.

Dr Potts introduced herself to Mary, but there was no response. She gave a succinct explanation of what she intended to do and detached the bag of saline from the needle in Mary's arm, and flushed the intravenous line with some distilled water from a syringe. In a seeming blur of activity, Mary's false teeth were removed, and a syringe of anaesthetic and then muscle relaxant injected down the venflon. Mary's frightened eyes closed. Her respiration hesitated and stopped. Dr Potts slipped in a short airway, and put a bag and mask over Mary's face and took over respiration. She satisfied herself that Mary was oxygenated and nodded to Power.

Dr Power dipped the foam discs of what looked like a pair of headphones into some salt solution, shook the padded electrodes free of drips and applied the foam electrodes to Mary's temples and flicked a switch. There was a buzzing from the machine itself for a few seconds and he pulled the electrodes away.

Dr Potts reapplied the mask and oxygen. Power pointed to Mary's hands. At first Sam could not see what he was pointing to. He beckoned her close and pointed again. She could just see a mild trembling of the fingers on both of Mary's hands. It was so brief, one moment it was there and then Mary's hands were still again.

Dr Potts looked at Mary's chest. She put a hand on her ribcage and reassured herself that Mary was beginning to breathe again. The anaesthetic was quickly wearing off now. Gently, Dr Potts turned Mary over into the recovery position. "There you go Mary," she said. The nurse took hold of Mary's hand and held it.

Power looked out of the window. The green of the trees and grass outside were more a sort of blue under the heavy sky. 'The clouds could hold snow,' he thought, 'if it were cold enough'. His thought ran back to a Christmas five years before when it had snowed. Power was happier these days, he thought, or was he?

Power turned to Sam. "Work done," he said. "Time for home. We'll probably give another treatment again on the 27th, after Boxing Day. I'm just hoping that the ECT restores Mary enough so that she can start to drink again."

"No Christmas dinner?" asked Sam.

Power chuckled. "If she can manage turkey and all the trimmings I'd be well pleased, but just at the moment I'd settle with her taking a bowl of porridge." He looked over at his patient. She was stirring and even struggling to sit upright.

Dr Potts, the anaesthetist, was clearing away and getting ready to go. The nurse was ringing for porters to take the patient back to the ward. In a few minutes the T clinic would be closed for Christmas. Power picked up his corduroy jacket from the chair and pulled it on.

He felt for his car keys in the pocket. It was getting very dark outside. "Let's head back home," he said to Sam.

Power was at the door, holding it open for Sam, when he turned to look at Mary. She was sitting up on the trolley and sipping some water from a plastic cup. She looked directly at Power and made eye contact. She held the cup up as if toasting him. Her face was still and sad, but she nodded. "Thank you, Dr Power."

Power smiled, and nodded back as he ushered Sam out of the clinic. He said, "Happy Christmas, Mary." And then he was gone into the night.

* * *

The journey from Cheadle to Alderley Edge in Power's battered Saab took around forty minutes. The winding road to Alderley was largely empty as people were settling down for their Christmas Eve. Sam hummed along to the cassette tape on the Saab's ancient stereo system. Power took pleasure in the bright red and yellow lights of the shop fronts as he motored through Alderley village. Power was looking out for the Piper, but he wasn't about this Christmas Eve.

Power turned left after the shops and revved the engine to climb the hill to the Edge.

The lights were blazing out of Alderley House in welcome as he turned the Saab between the sandstone pillars of his gates. He beamed at Sam as they halted. "A good day's work," he smiled. "I'm starving!"

The front door was open in welcome. Against the light were the familiar figures of his friend, Andrew Lynch, and his wife, Lynch's sister, Valerie, Lynch's nephew, Robert, Tim Jenkins from the Lion in Shrewsbury and his girlfriend, Claire. And Power's father was there, standing in front of the crowd, smiling, and with open arms.

Power sighed a sigh of happiness. The house was full for

Christmas. There was the happy prospect of good food, wine and good company ahead.

Epilogue: Journey's End
or
The Pavilion
March 1998

Power had requested a few days leave from his new hospital to form a long weekend and had booked accommodation in the country to help him relax. At the last moment he had gathered enough courage to ask a friend along and Power had been pleased and surprised that the response had been so affirmative.

He travelled alone on Friday morning. He had planned to take the green Saab, but it had refused to leave the garage. Power chose another of what was now his current stable of Saabs; a red one that seemed more willing to serve. He had risen early and set off before the rush hour infiltrated the day. He avoided the motorways and took the old A roads southwest through Cheshire and down on the A49 intending to enjoy the Spring countryside of Shropshire. He drove relatively slowly taking in the views over the fields and stopping occasionally to view the older villages. At Whitchurch he turned right onto the A495 and breezed past hedgerows and the ancient Whixall Mosses to the small market town of Ellesmere. He stopped there to sip a takeaway coffee as he walked the only few streets there were, to stretch his legs. He retraced his path slightly, passing Ellesmere's Mere for the second time and headed right on the A528 past Blakemere and Whitemere, towards Cockshutt and Burlton. He then detoured, to a find a pub recommended to him by Superintendent Lynch, and went a few miles east to the village of

Ruyton XI Towns. Power parked his Saab in the pub car park until it opened, and took a walk up the hill towards the Saxon church. As he walked through the sleepy graveyard he looked at the inscriptions on the old headstones and found delight in the sight of grass, moist from a recent shower glistening in the sun, and shining cobwebs bedecked with sparking droplets of fallen rain. Beside the church stood the toothstump remnants of a castle. A board placed by the ruins informed Power that it had been built by John le Strange in the 12th Century. He read that once the tiny village had been the centre of eleven towns. Power nodded to himself and wandered in the sun, feeling the muscles of his whole upper body relax now he was away from work. He let out a great sigh of contentment and relaxation which he was glad no-one else could hear.

Feeling a thirst for a holiday celebration pint of beer, he began to descend the hill. As he walked along the deserted street he remembered what Lynch had told him of the village. He recalled Lynch had mentioned that Conan Doyle, the author, had worked as a young assistant here a few years before he had started writing about Sherlock Holmes. Lynch had reported Conan Doyle's joke that Ruyton was "not big enough to make one town, far less eleven".

The 'Talbot' pub was opening up, and Power ordered a pint of Joules' ale and an egg and cress sandwich. He sat outside in the Spring day's sun and admired the village before him.

After quaffing down a third of a pint, Dr Power reached into his jacket pocket for a well-thumbed copy of *Dr Pascal* by Zola. He had first read the novel when he was at Medical School. In those days he had liked the theme of science challenging religion and Dr Pascal's hope that his lifework would unravel the genetics that both strengthened and weakened his family. The religious challenge to Dr Pascal's work, from within his own family, had seemed incomprehensible to the twenty year old Carl Power. The theme of tension between religion and science had been well rehearsed in arguments in the pub with his friend, Andrew Lynch. Although nowadays his friend's fervour about religion seemed an anachronism in an increasingly secular Western world. It almost seemed that Science had won. Against this background Power wondered why he had let Lynch persuade him to accompany him on his future planned journey to Northern Spain to walk the St James' Way to Santiago. He opened the book, as a couple of girls on horseback clopped lazily by the 'Talbot' pub. Power had read perhaps a dozen pages of the old book when his phone rang.

The pub window by Power's head was open, and the barmaid inside listened as Power conversed on the phone. Tantalisingly, she could hear only one side of the conversation; Power's deep voice.

"Yes, of course . . . looking forward to seeing you, so much. Do you know what time you will get there? Seven-ish? Okay. Safe drive . . . Okay. I'll be waiting."

The barmaid noticed that the customer was smiling broadly when he came inside to order a second pint.

"You look happy," she said, probing.

"Yep," said Power, giving nothing away. He felt a pleasurable anxiety due to eager anticipation, but he didn't let that show either. He tried to order and pay for a flat white coffee, but this was not the city and term 'flat white coffee' drew a blank look. A black filter coffee was negotiated instead. Power returned outside into the glowing afternoon and sat down again to read from Dr Pascal. The good doctor, researching into heredity and battling against the religious sensibilities of his own family, was the subject of loving criticism by his eighty year old mother who said: "Science. A fine thing science, that goes against all that is most sacred in the world! When they shall have demolished everything they will have advanced greatly! They kill respect, they kill the family, they kill the good God!" Power sipped his coffee and mused. The first time he had read the novel as a medical student he had sided completely with Dr Pascal and his assertion of scientific rationality against the stifling inertia of his family's religion. Now, in the sun, Power thought of his friend, Lynch, and his resolute faith. How the tide had changed in favour of secularity since Zola had written his novel at the end of the nineteenth century. Science rather than religion was the dogma at the last gasp of the twentieth century. It was Lynch and other believers that seemed to be outsiders pitted against orthodoxy now. In contrast to his student self did the eminently qualified Dr Power still side with Dr Pascal? As Dr Pascal would have it did Dr Power share the opinion that there was only one possible belief – a belief in life – life as the only divine manifestation.

Power drained his coffee, struggled for an instant to remember if he had paid for everything, then set off for his car, which was parked near the old stable block at the rear of The Talbot.

Travelling eastward, driving with speedy care, through the country lanes and B roads of Shropshire and Staffordshire Power edged ever closer to his destination, the village of Ingestre. Just north of a market town he turned the Saab hard left and onto a private lane. He passed a corner plot house, then an open barn with cows wandering lazily between their shelter and the fields beyond, corralled in safety by cattle grids which Power rumbled across. Five hundred yards further on he passed a yard with an unattended, vast and gently smouldering charcoal burner.

Suddenly he passed from brilliant white sunshine into a wash of lime and emerald green light filtering through a high canopy of oak and beech leaves, as the Saab shot into the forest.

Power slowed to a halt to allow his eyes to adjust and also to check the map he had been sent in the post. Reassured he was on the right track he moved off and turned a left hand bend. An avenue through the trees stretched out in front of him. The relative darkness under the forest canopy stretched as far as the eye could see down the avenue, except for a small arch of sunlight in the distance where the forest ended and sunlit fields could be glimpsed. Here, in the semi-darkness Power had reached journey's end. Halfway down the avenue was a classical eighteenth century portico with a triangular pediment atop four columns. Power turned the Saab into the parking place by the Pavilion and switched off the engine.

All at once the silence of the forest descended upon Power like a heavy green velvet curtain separating the doctor from the frantic world beyond. He got out of the car and wandered around the Pavilion looking for the place where the housekeeper had told him the key would be hidden. He kept on seeing new things; an enclosed garden with neatly trimmed lawn behind the Pavilion, a bank of ground elder and nettles that bounded the back of the property, and a gentle sloped vista in front of the road by the pavilion densely carpeted with bluebells, with a field and the bottom of the slope dotted with tiny white blobs which could only be sheep. He found the key hidden, as had been promised by the housekeeper on the phone, in a dummy birdbox at head height on the trunk of a nearby oak tree.

Power inserted the key in the lock of one of the doors under the vast pediment and opened it. A waft of the internal air moved past him smelling of wood polish and home. He entered the stillness and opened internal doors on a ground floor bedroom, a kitchen and downstairs bathroom and a vast hexagonal open living space that was two storey's high. The room was lined by shelves of books. A balustrade walkway made a kind of minstrel's gallery opposite the windows. A stone fireplace had been set with twigs and logs by the housekeeper. With satisfaction Power noted a full basket of logs by a pale blue wingback armchair. He fell back, full length, onto the red cushions of a four seater sofa and stared up at the ceiling high above him.

Stirring himself, he unloaded food and wine from the Saab, stocked the fridge up, put the kettle on for tea and lit the living room fire. Nursing a mug of tea in both hands, he sat on the sofa and watched the flames of the fire flicker into life.

With the fire established against the cool of the gathering dusk outside, Power took his leather holdall of clothes upstairs. There was a headless statue at the top of the stairs, which seemed somewhat ominous, and he resolved to keep the lights on all night. There were two upstairs bedrooms; one twin room and, across the Minstrel's gallery, another room with a squeaky double bed and adjoining bathroom. The bathroom windows looked up and down the empty private road outside.

Power's stomach rumbled and he looked at his watch. Would she be here soon or should he eat? In this remote spot, far from civilisation, his mobile had no signal. He plugged in a radio that he had packed. It crackled into life and filled the lofty space of the living room with Classical Sound.

In the kitchen he listened to strains of the music that drifted through to him. He made himself an omelette and ate on his own, with bread and salad. He opened a bottle of Jamelles Viognier, but drank only one glass. He kept looking at his watch and disconsolately thought of the women he had lost; Eve and Lucinda. The hour was getting late. Maybe she wasn't coming after all? The mobile still resolutely displayed no signal.

The windows were blue with dusk, and Power switched on the lights inside and outside.

He went to the front door several times and stared into the gathering gloom.

For want of something to do he picked up a torch and going

outside, trudged down the hill, feeling the thick carpet of bluebells brush his ankles as he strode. In the dark he almost stumbled down a haha, but just in time the oval light beam of the torch picked out the declivity and he jumped across the void.

He was moving downward through a cleared swathe of meadow, and on both sides were tall trees and dense forest. He reached the bottom of the long slope and his progress was stalled by a double row of barbed wire. The sheep that had been in the field beyond had disappeared from view. The air felt cool and smelt fresh.

Power turned and looked back.

The Pavilion and its columns were illuminated against the navy blue marbled night sky. It looked a long way away. Power suddenly felt uneasy, alone. As an experiment he switched the torch off and the shadow engulfed him. As suddenly as the light disappeared, suppressed memories of the cave under Alderley House gathered around and clawed at, gnawed at, his consciousness. There was a crack of a twig in the woods at his right, and Power suddenly formed the fearful idea that he had been followed by somebody in the woods, step by step, as he descended the slope. He imagined he had heard their steps but somehow ignored them. Heard their breathing, but somehow discounted the warning.

There was a rustle as someone moved stealthily through the undergrowth towards Power.

His finger paused on the torch switch.

Power was petrified. Unable to act.

A long second. His finger pressed down on the switch and the torch light burned incandescently bright.

Two bright pinpoints of light shone at him from the dark wood. *Tapetum lucidem.*

The fox stared back at Power, its eyes burning fiercely white, reflecting his torch. Lazily, the fox turned and trotted off through the bluebells and Power breathed freely again.

Power ran back up the slope towards the warmth and safety of the Pavilion. As he did so, he heard a car's engine and the spatter of tyres on the stones of the gravelled drive. Power saw car headlights washing over the green crowns of the trees and shining between the tree trunks. Her car swung into the parking space beside Power's.

And all at once she was there; climbing out of her Old English white Mini and falling into his arms. Power clasped her to him, gladly hugging her in her bright red woollen coat and nuzzling into her soft blonde hair. "So pleased you made it," Power said.

"Were you waiting out here?"

"I'd just been down to the edge of the woods," said Power. "And there was a fox following me."

"You must have scared him, poor little thing."

"It was me that was scared, not he." Power retrieved her small case from the boot and they went indoors.

She looked up at the columns and carved portico with admiration. "And this is all ours? The wood too?"

"For the weekend, yes. All ours. A splendid exile from the world."

"Indeed," she smiled at him and stroked his face. Her eyes met his and were full of love. Power wondered why he had ever taken so long to understand.

"I've opened a bottle and made a fire," said Power drawing her into the Pavilion's heart. She looked round approvingly at the comfortable chairs and the rug in front of the crackling fire. She shed her coat, like an old skin and stood anew in front of him. He could not help but kiss her, slowly this time. They sank onto the vast sofa and for a while they were entwined and, for each other, ravenous. They surfaced and both drank wine, smiling madly at each other and bubbling with laughter, until she grew serious.

"We have something to celebrate, Carl Power. I'm proud of you!"

"Why?" said Power puzzled.

"There was a call today. A follow up on a letter you once wrote. Do you remember the soldier? And that dreadful officer that visited him and took him out of your care?"

Carl remembered something, but dimly. "Jones?"

"That was it, Private Jones. And you were so annoyed when the Colonel, Arkshaw, misquoted you. Jones was charged with absence and illegal possession of firearms, court martialled, imprisoned, discharged and lost his pension. And you didn't let matters rest. You wrote to the Ministry."

"I remember, but that was years ago."

"I remember too," she said. "You were so cross. There has been an investigation because you complained. And a Colonel in the Military Police phoned the hospital today to tell you what happened." Power took a glug of wine and raised an inquisitive eyebrow. "Colonel Arkshaw was investigated. He's done the same thing several times. Made out that ill people he didn't like were well, and the other way round – even taken money from some others to get them pensions for illnesses he faked. Like Jones, who had PTSD. Instead of treating them he got them dismissed or imprisoned. Arkshaw just liked power and let it go to his head."

"So he's lost his job?" Power began to feel a twinge of guilt.

"More than that, he's been charged and imprisoned himself. Somewhere like Colchester, I think. Dishonourably discharged. And the GMC will strike him off."

"Should we be celebrating?" Power didn't like to think of bringing misfortune down on anyone.

"Yes," she said and her eyes burned with certainty. "Jones has got an ill-health pension back. And some other soldiers have had their commissions re-instated. So you made a difference. Arkshaw was a monster, Carl. He deserved what he got. Jones had been living rough on the streets for years. Putting that right – that is worth some celebration!" And she poured them some more wine. They raised them in a toast and drank their glasses dry. "My hero," she grinned and hugged him. "Now, it's late, are you going to take me upstairs to bed?"

"All right, Laura," he stood and held out his arm and together, hand in hand, they wended their way to the foot of the stairs.

Commentary for Dr Power's Case Book

Some collections of short stories begin with a well-meant introduction, which includes a commentary and notes on the various stories. I have decided to place this commentary at the end of the book to avoid the difficulties inherent in such introductions – which can slow down the beginning of the book and also reveal key elements of the plots.

Dr Power's Case Book grew as a concept as I answered the various questions sent to me from readers of the first three Dr Power novels. Readers wanted to know what happened in the world of Dr Power between the novels; about his life, his patients and his friends. What happened to his girlfriend Eve who was in the first novel? What happened in the case of Mr Hammadi? Whatever happened to the children of Sir Ian McWilliam? This collection aims to answer some of these questions, and also provides some links and hidden clues to the rest of the mysteries in the series.

The book was never intended to have a thriller format although three of the stories do have some mystery elements (**Magpies, The Artist,** and **The Farm**). The book is meant to flesh out the world of Dr Power and Superintendent Lynch for real fans.

I have written a few notes on each story and also show in the table below where each story fits chronologically into the sequence of novels.

Any story might feature a detail of Dr Power's medical career, or a short-story sized mystery, but each story features a medical diagnosis, which tallies with the theme of this being a doctor's casebook, and each diagnosis might form either a major or a minor element of the story. As a starter, Christmas 1993 revolves around the diagnosis of **Post Traumatic Stress Disorder.** I will leave the reader to fathom out the other diagnoses.

The stories are designed to be read singly and stand alone, but they also build up a narrative over time.

Timeline: The sequence of Dr Power stories

Time -Story

1993 Summer - - - - The Darkening Sky (novel)

1993 December - - - - - - - - - - - -Christmas 1993

1994 March 13th - - - - - - - - - - - - - - - - Delirium

1994 June -The Dark

1994 Summer - - - - - - The Fire of Love (novel)

1994 September - - - - - - - - - - - - - -The Soldier

1994 September - - - - - - - - - - - - -The Scissors

1994 October - - - - - - - - - - - - - - - - -The Porche

1994 December - - - - - - -The Shooting Range

1995 February - - - - - - - - - - - - - - - - - -The Artist

1996 May - The Farm

1996 June 16/17th - - - - - - - - - -The Fallen Man

1997 March - - - - - - - - - - - - - - - -Magpies (Eliza)

1997 April - - - - - - - - - - - - - - - - - -The Unmother

1997 Summer - - - The Good Shepherd (novel)

1997 December - - - - - - - - - - - -Christmas 1997

1998 March - - - - - - - - - - - - - - - - -Journey's End

1998 - - - - - - - - - - - - -Schrödinger's God (novel)

Notes on the stories:

Christmas 1993 – This first story takes up Power's life a few months after the events of **The Darkening Sky.** The story has a rather lonely feel to it and explains what happened to Power and his artist girlfriend, Eve. Both endured traumatic events in the first novel and I thought that this would undoubtedly have an impact on the couple.

Delirium – Dr Power stories are generally set in the North West of England. Power trained around Liverpool, but in the first three books practices as a Consultant Psychiatrist in Cheshire, living in the well-to-do area of Alderley Edge. For this story he returns to his training hospital, The Royal Liverpool University Hospital as a locum consultant. He reveals himself as a rather detached follower of football and is called in to see a patient who has absconded from the ward whilst disorientated. He follows the patient into a dangerous eyrie and talks her down, demonstrating an everyday kind of heroism that arguably means much more to society than an epic kind of heroism. The story also features a character Roly, the Porter, who makes his first appearance in **The Fire of Love,** after a job move.

There is reference to Power's grandfather, a lifelong supporter of Liverpool FC, and his grandson's very tentative relationship to the club as a supporter. This is Power's first attendance at Anfield and it is Derby Day. The match report for the actual day states: 'The match fizzed and crackled from start to stupendous finish when, with seconds left, the Liverpool goalkeeper, James, produced the save of the match to deny Everton an injury-time equaliser.' Power only manages to see the first half as he is called away, but he is surprised by the emotion of being immersed in the stadium experience and reminded of his own involvement at Hillsborough insofar as he treated the survivors on their way back to the city.

Dr Power is usually a very careful historian as he knows that most diagnoses are based on the patient's history, and that most errors of negligence follow a slapdash approach to the discipline of history taking. He is mildly appalled to learn that the junior doctors in Mrs Carey's case have neglected to consider an alcohol history. It could be that they thought Mrs Carey was an unlikely candidate for a regular tipple, but people are a constant source of surprises. A proper alcohol history might have forewarned them about the possibility of delirium after admission. However, sometimes people with alcohol problems do have a tendency to minimize their intake.

The Dark – is set in Power's own home in Alderley Edge. In the books the house is Alderley House, a Victorian home in Alderley Edge supposedly designed by Waterhouse – who was a famous North Western architect who designed Manchester Town Hall and the Natural History Museum in London – his work is featured elsewhere in the Dr Power novels – his fictional designs include Heaton Hall in **The Fire of Love**. **The Dark** is a literal journey into the fabric of the Edge itself, and a allegorical descent into Power's unconscious. There has been a previous allusion to this aspect of Jungian psychology in **The Darkening Sky**. There are some hidden elements in this story that will be picked up in a later novel. Afficionados may have noted that the cavern below Alderley House is featured on the cover for **The Dr Power Mysteries** (a compendium of the first three novels).

The Soldier – is set soon after **The Fire of Love** and details the kind of upsetting clash that doctors can have over diagnoses and management. These are unpleasant events in a doctor's life, but can be devastating for a patient. Power's secretary, Laura, hopes that Power can exert aspects of his everyday heroism to right the injustice served up to his patient.

The Scissors – details the anxieties that a doctor like Dr Power can have about a patient, their safety and the safety of others and about how it can sometimes be a battle just to do the right thing. There is a classical allusion to Greek myth and fate embedded in the story.

The Porsche – is set in Wilmslow, near Power's home and hospital practice. Power is called to a crisis where a patient of his colleague's has caused devastation to a garage. The story features the larger than life, Rubici Hammadi, who previously appeared in **The Darkening Sky.** Hammadi has 'flight of ideas' and also describes a literal flight into a garage in his disinhibition. His speech is highly characteristic of mania with rhyming associations, here based on his doctor's name – "Free as a bird . . . to fly . . . how we flew Dr Power! Flying power, flower power, self raising flour power!"

In his destruction of highly desirable objects of consumerism Mr Hammadi quotes from Shakespeare's *Timon of Athens:* 'For bounty, that makes gods, does still mar men. My dearest lord, bless'd, to be most accursed, Rich, only to be wretched, thy great fortunes; Are made thy chief afflictions.'

The Shooting Range – features Superintendent Lynch and Sergeant Beresford and documents Lynch's attempt to have Power trained to defend himself. if necessary, with firearms. Power is less than enthusiastic. Lynch's effort is more to do with managing his own anxiety for his friend's wellbeing after experiences in **The Darkening Sky** and **The Fire of Love**. Lynch may be aiming to bolster Power's self-confidence rather than promote the use of guns. Unfortunately, there are unforeseen events in the Shooting Range that require Power's medical training. Power is trained to use a Glock. A Glock also makes a key appearance in **The Good Shepherd.**

The Artist – when I set to writing the stories I thought Eve only would manifest once in the first story, but she clearly wanted to be in another. This is a sort of mystery story, although more of a psychological puzzle about the nature of art and forgery, and what might drive an artist to forge other people's work. Dr Power is joined by Superintendent Lynch to resolve the issue.

The Farm – This describes what happened to Power's would-be girlfriend Lucinda McWilliam and her errant brother after the events in **The Fire of Love.** Both Lucinda and her brother are effectively transformed by the virtually simultaneous deaths of their mother and father. The transformation is not a fortuitous one, and in order to keep their father's estate, they develop a burgeoning enterprise behind the locked gates of Heaton Hall, which falls foul of the law. Cannabis farms are big business and the seclusion of Heaton Hall seems ideal, but Power's encounter with Lucinda in town after a play means that he tries to contact her again and this threatens her new *status quo.*

There is a dilemma consequent upon Power's discovery of the cannabis farm. What should he do after discovering the farm at Heaton Hall. If he talks to his friend, Lynch, he betrays any residual affection he had for Lucinda. If he doesn't alert Lynch is he perforce complicit in the illegal enterprise and jeopardising his friendship with Lynch? What do you think Power should have done?

The story is set at a specific time in Manchester and reader's can themselves investigate and conjecture about the sinister white van that Power notices.

The Fallen Man – The time setting of this story is also significant as it falls on a specific day in Dublin's literary calendar and is itself played out in the span of 24 hours. Power's work as a medicolegal expert is a recurrent feature in the novels. He sometimes spars with his apparent nemesis, consultant psychiatrist, Professor Anastasi, who opposed Power in Court in **The Fire of Love.** In this story Power is asked to give evidence in a personal injury case and flies in to a relaxed city in permanent party mode. The case involves a man who fell from a window, but is it Power who is really the fallen man. Uncharacteristically, Power has a rather frenzied evening before he is due to give evidence. He is caught up in the atmosphere of the bars, drinks Power's Whiskey (it's real – try the 12 year Special Reserve if you can), and falls in with a young English Postgraduate from Trinity College and has an encounter of the closest sort. As fate has it though, he loses his new friend's details in the Liffey and is brim-full of regret as he flies out 24 hours after his arrival.

Of course, the story containment within the boundary of 24 hours is a nod to James Joyce's *Ullysses*. However, I was also minded of the notion of 24 hours as a metaphor for life.

In the 1990 novel, *Jurassic Park,* by the excellent Michael Crichton, the Chaos mathematician Ian Malcolm expounds upon the chaos within a day:

'A day is like a whole life. You start out doing one thing, but end up doing something else, plan to run an errand, but never get there . . . . And at the end of your life, your whole existence has that same haphazard quality, too. Your whole life has the same shape as a single day.'

Magpies (Eliza) – I should emphasise that this story is fictional or conjectural in nature. There is a counting theme to the story – with reference to the ancient, superstition-riddled rhyme about magpies. This is often quoted as:

One for sorrow,
Two for joy,
Three for a girl,
Four for a boy,
Five for silver,
Six for gold,
Seven for a secret,
Never to be told.

I recommend the haunting version incorporated in the song *The Magpie* by *The Unthanks.*

Counting rituals can be compulsive behaviours, symptomatic of underlying obsessional thinking which exists to help keep some anxiety at bay. In this story, Eliza uses numbers to ward off her deep seated and enduring anxieties about the death of her employer. I must emphasise that the story is a fiction based on some historical elements, but many of the facts in the story are true. The reader is invited to research the details of Magpies and see which ones are included in historical accounts of the life and death of Alan Turing. His post mortem details are available on-line. Details of his will are also available to researchers. Turing did live not far from Power's fictional house. He did have a housekeeper called Eliza who did discover his body. He left her £30 annually, but I have extrapolated some feelings to Eliza, which are purely my interpretation. Did she believe in the theory of his suicide, or believe otherwise. She did not describe depression in her employer, whom she saw most days, and her relationship was not simply that of a cleaner. She cooked for him and noted he ate his lamb chops on the night before his death. Had Turing wished to kill himself, perhaps might he not have left a note downstairs to prevent his employee going upstairs and being distressed at finding him dead?

The conventional wisdom is that Turing killed himself in apparent disgrace following a conviction for then – illegal sexual activity. However, the conviction had been two years prior to his death. It is unlikely that we will have any alternative official explanation to the existing conventional one. Turing's last few years are an interesting puzzle, however.

Turing was very interested in the idea of artificial intelligence. We have him to thank for the Turing test, which Wikipedia defines as a *'test of a machine's ability to exhibit intelligent behavior equivalent to, or indistinguishable from, that of a human'.*

The Eliza program was designed between 1964 and 1966 by Dr Weizenbaum. It is a simple simulation of a Rogerian psychotherapy session. Dr Rogers was a psychotherapist who ironically espoused person centred therapy and practiced unconditional positive regard. Coincidentally, Dr Rogers's first name is Carl, like Dr Power's first name. The program is available on-line and is quite remarkable in its ability to seemingly respond appropriately to typed in comments. Try it.

As an additional coincidence, the computer program that Turing would probably have loved is called Eliza, and so actually was his housekeeper, Eliza Clayton. Newspaper reports of the time, documenting Turing's Inquest, refer to middle class neighbours by name, but do not give Eliza a name and merely refer to her as 'a housekeeper', or 'a cleaner'. I think she was important.

The Unmother – Severe mental illness such as profound depression or delusional schizophrenia can lead to neglect or even direct harm of a child. This is, of course, a tragedy for all concerned. Psychiatrists, such as Dr Power, can understand such maternal behaviour in the context of mental illness, and seek to prevent harm. In this story, however, Dr Power struggles to find a mental illness that can explain the neglect of a child by a mother, and the mood of the professionals concerned seems to be one of deep frustration or even anger with the mother. Is this reaction by staff acceptable, or not? Dr Power is presented with a person who can seemingly simulate depression when he examines her, but observations by nursing staff suggest that this mood is being feigned to enlist his sympathy. This might suggest an abnormal personality, rather than illness. Power loses sympathy with his patient, (especially after he is confronted with pictures of the child, Kyle, which the police insist he views, possibly in a manipulative attempt to break any sympathy he has for his patient).

Dr Power spars once more with his medicolegal nemesis, Professor Anastasi, who is content to take what the mother says at face value and diagnose depression.

Is it acceptable for health professionals to react emotionally to patients, to judge mothers and their behaviour? Which doctor is right? Or are they both wrong?

Christmas 1997 – Dr Power takes the opportunity to teach a potential medical student, Sam, Lynch's niece, who first appeared in **The Good Shepherd.** The piece features a patient whom Power treats with electroconvulsive treatment or ECT. ECT is an effective treatment for severe depression, but it has fallen out of favour in recent times, and is increasingly difficult to source. ECT was invented by Ugo Cerletti and team in the 1930s, and was the first effective treatment for depression. Power explains the treatment and attempts to correct any misperceptions that Sam has. Psychological treatment for depression is perceived as more acceptable by the public and some mental health professionals. Unfortunately, psychotherapy is simply not effective in severe depression and even in milder depression only works slightly better than placebo. The thing is, that everyone hopes that psychotherapy will work – both practitioners and patients, and maybe this clouds society's judgement regarding the place for psychotherapy. Effective treatment for moderate to severe depression, an eminently treatable disorder, is frustratingly becoming less easy to find. This is a shame, as our society should be becoming more enlightened and effective treatment for more severe depression should be easily available.

Journey's End – prefigures the fourth Dr Power novel, **Schrödinger's God** and is intended to set the scene for a scenario that will challenge the mettle and faith of both Dr Power and Superintendent Lynch. The two Christmas stories were meant to be like bookends for the Casebook – depicting contrasting Christmases for Power – the early one being a sad and lonely affair and the later one filled with optimism and the promise of good friends and their company. However, the story **The Soldier** demanded some just resolution, and I wanted to settle Power down for a bit in a more successful and enduring relationship. There have been many hints along the way that Laura had significant feelings for Dr Power. For instance if Laura didn't have these feelings then why did she mind *so* very much when he resigned in **The Good Shepherd?** And despite supposedly being a successful psychiatrist, Power never really picked up the clues. Perhaps we can forgive him for being obtuse in personal matters – sometimes it isn't always easy to see what is right under your nose. Laura also has the fun of telling Dr Power that justice has finally been done for his patient.

If the reader has any questions, then please do pose these on Goodreads.com where Hugh Greene is featured. Alternatively, please contact him about your favourite story via the website www.hughgreene.com

Music for Dr Power's Casebook

A set of music has been suggested by readers; these suggestions accompany some of the music that inspired the author, Hugh Greene, whilst writing the original novels.

If you would like to suggest additions to this list please email the author via www.hughgreene.com

The Music, the Album if relevant, and the Artist:

Tranquility —— Tranquility —— Direct

Eve's Volcano —— Saint Julian —— Julian Cope

Pierce —— Pierced —— David Lang

Nothing is Something Worth Doing —— Ineffable Mysteries —— Shpongle

The Great Outdoors —— Series of Ands —— Wim Mertens

Flower of The Mountain —— Director's Cut —— Kate Bush

Delirium Waltz —— Retro Lounge —— Vono Box

Dublin Rocks —— A Toast to Irish Music —— Andy Lock

Falling Slowly —— Music from Once —— Glen Hansard & Marketa Irglova

Paper Scissors Stone —— Isla —— Portico Quartet

Digital Psychiatry —— Digital Psychiatry —— Magnosis

Neglected Fixations —— Neglected Fixations —— Syncopix

Thirty Pieces of Silver —— It's Not Me —— Janice Graham Band

Nimrod —— Enigma Variations —— Elgar

Turing / Sequence —— Wilderness —— Makeup and Vanity Set

Elegy for Dunkirk —— Atonement —— Dario Marianelli

Chasing Sheep is Best Left to Shepherds —— Michael Nyman

Sudden Throw —— For Now I am Winter —— Olafur Arnalds

Sandstone —— A State of Trance —— Rex Mundi

Midnight —— Lights in the Sky —— Peter Gregson

Beautiful Mechanical —— Beautiful Mechanical —— Ryan Lott

Green's Leaves —— Chambers —— Chilly Gonzales

You'll Never Walk Alone —— Gerry and the Pacemakers
Lenny Valentino —— Now I'm a Cowboy —— The Auteurs
Invention a 2 Voix No. 13 —— Days to Come —— Jacques Loussier
Solid Air —— Solid Air —— John Martyn
Apache —— Incredible Bongo Band
Elegia —— Low Life —— New Order
Blue Monday —— Singles —— New Order
Rose Hip November —— Just Another Diamond Day —— Vashti Bunyan
Rue Des templates —— L'eu Rouge —— The Young Gods
Freestyler —— In Stereo —— Bomfunk MCs
Toccata & Fugue in D Minor —— Just Play Vol 1 —— Jacques Loussier
The Clown —— Portraits —— Maribou State
Butterfly —— Don't Get Weird on Me —— Lloyd Cole
Dead Format —— Dumb Flesh —— Blanck Mass
Young Persons Guide to the Orchestra —— Benjamin Britten
The Killing Moon —— Songs to Learn and Sing —— Echo and the Bunnymen
The Fly —— Fegmaniel —— Robyn Hitchcock
Ghosts VIP —— Tsar Bombe —— Bisweed
Night Scare —— Sticks —— Chris Joss
You've Been Spiked —— You've Been Spiked —— Chris Joss
Shooting the Moon In the Eye —— Shooting the Moon —— Killda Brain
The Dark Matters —— A State of Trance —— Sied van Riel
Morpheus Miracle Maker —— I a moon —— North Sea Radio Orchestra
Requiem in D Minor —— Requiem —— Mozart
Brandenburg 5 —— Concerto —— Bach
Raven —— Raven —— Helena
Down in the Woods —— Standing at the Sky's Edge —— Richard Hawley
Last Lullaby —— Mount the Air —— The Unthanks
Magpie —— Mount the Air —— The Unthanks
Cloud of the Unknowing —— Cognessence —— Robert Logan
The Angel — The Cloud of Unknowing — Cloud

Wond'ring — Aloud — Aqualing — Jethro Tull

Year of the Dragon — Year of the Dragon — yMusic

Follow the Light — Sub Focus — Sub Focus

Symphony in E Flat — Haydn

Man of the World — Fleetwood Mac — Fleetwood Mac

Legions (War) — One Cello x 16 — Zoe Keating

Schrödinger —— Noise in Sepher —— Anakronic Electro Orchestra

Recomposed: Vivaldi —— Recomposed —— Max Richter

Infra 2 ——Max Richter

Printed in Great Britain
by Amazon